No Brakes

The Fiction of Lois Gould

Medusa's Gift

Subject to Change

La Presidenta

X: A Fabulous Child's Story

A Sea-Change

Final Analysis

Necessary Objects

Such Good Friends

NO BRAKES

A NOVEL

Lois Gould

A Marian Wood Book

Henry Holt and Company
New York

Henry Holt and Company, Inc.
Publishers since 1866
115 West 18th Street
New York, New York 10011

Henry Holt® is a registered trademark of
Henry Holt and Company, Inc.

Published in Canada by Fitzhenry & Whiteside Ltd.,
195 Allstate Parkway, Markham, Ontario L3R 4T8.

Library of Congress Cataloging-in-Publication Data
Gould, Lois.
No brakes: a novel/
by Lois Gould.—1st ed.
p.   cm.
"A Marian Wood book."
I. Title.
PS3557.087N6   1997   96-25523
813'.54—dc20   CIP
ISBN 0-8050-4117-6

Henry Holt books are available for special promotions
and premiums. For details contact: Director, Special Markets.

First Edition—1997

Designed by KELLY SOONG

Printed in the United States of America
All first editions are printed on acid-free paper. ∞

1   3   5   7   9   10   8   6   4   2

Shoot the women first. They are the last to take up arms, and the last to lay them down.

—PRECEPT OF SAS
(SPECIAL ARMED SERVICES, BRITAIN'S
ANTITERRORISM COMMANDO FORCE)

To Tony, with love.
Roger and the B., always.
Also to T.C.W.—One for the Road

Acknowledgments

The author wishes to thank The Writers Room in New York, whose haven afforded shelter for this work in its final stages. Thanks, too, to Constance W. Aldridge, whose support and friendship sustained both the author and the book at Mount Falcon Castle, Ballina, County Mayo, Ireland.

NO BRAKES

O N E

~⌣~

Ludo in red. His terrible beauty rushes up like flame from the soft rolled silk. The neck bared, eyes shadow-playing; a face you would rather stare at from a safe distance, or from inside a vivid wine dream. But here he is, loosely wrapped in this handful of lustrous crimson, careless as an extravagant gift, possibly stolen.

Does he think of this effect, as he tugs absently at the edges of silk that do not meet, quite; that slip away at his touch, exposing another sliver of him, as though this is an old sly game between them?

His mouth shines with wine. Consider that mouth, soft and full; the lower lip with a sort of cleft in its center, a pause, a lay-by for the tip of a tongue, someone's tongue, or teeth. The mouth sucks at its wine from a huge stemmed glass, wine darker than the sliding silk of that robe of his, no less intoxicating.

Ludo in black, at 130 miles per hour, profile etched against flying trees, mysterious streaming shadows. The mouth now soft as sleep after sex, the mouth of a baby after suckling; droplets of milk still warm at the corners. Ludo feeds it tenderly: a finger, a cigarette, icy rim of a cola can. Alternating sensations of wet, harsh, sweet. I hum: *Can't get no . . . Satisfaction . . .* He doesn't hear me. He is listening to other music, his ears boxed by violent cuffs of sound. At this pitch, this speed, any music he selects is a cry of sexual pain. Ecstatic. *You drive me crazy . . . uh-huh.* There is of course no "you." He is alone, hurtling. He has lost touch with the road, lost touch. Except for his body, swaddled in the red car's carnal embrace. It holds him fast in its black leather lap; dominatrix. As though it is taking him silently from behind. A favorite position for married sex partners, or spoons in a hope chest.

At the end of this midnight ride, Ludo emerges like a dazed Lothario, eyes still caressing the dazzling mistress that lets him go without reproach. He and the car shine together like danger in the wet, silent street. Gypsy dancers drenched after the tarantelle, that ancient whirling madness that was either a cure or only a sign of the fatal malady. He stands gazing. His passport, cards of identity, licenses to drive, may all slip silently from his breast pocket into the glistening market square of a town midway between destinations. Walking away, he would not notice that for the moment he had ceased to exist.

Ludo in bed. Arms naked, flung backward, curving upward; an odalisque's languid pose. He wakes smiling at something he knew an instant before waking, before I entered the room, before he realized I was there, transfixed like an animal caught in high beams.

Or was it, that smile, meant for me after all? I cannot look away from the vulnerable angle of arms, the modeled smoothness, the sweet underline. I lurch; not all of me, of course, not visibly. I catch my breath, cover, recover. Standing there is a sudden ride, vertical, vertiginous, too steep, in a dodgem car. I stammer something, anything. Our eyes are strangers locked in this intimate space. The rest of his torso is mummy-wrapped in pale blue sheets. But his waking face still smiles, it seems truly now, at me. He knows. Does he?

Today we are going for another kind of ride. Not in the beautiful red car this time, but the silver. Equally beautiful. This one is mine. Well, not exactly. Here's your car, he had said to me one starry midnight, a year before. Yours to crash, he said, if you need to. But of course it was his, really.

I drove it to distraction, as terrified of it as of him. Now we are co-drivers. A team. Want to? he asked. Historic race. Northern Ireland. Tests, time controls, passage checks, penalties. Your car or mine? You could write about it.

Imagine: lost with Ludo at high speed, in mountain passes, darkness, ditches, dirt paths cut like tunnels beneath arching hedgerows. Rain, mist, trouble, unapproved roads. In Northern Ireland, he explains, the Unapproved Road is plainly marked, with a black arrow to make the point. Drive on, and you will be shot. I take it figuratively. All my pleasures are ill-advised. Want to? He asks. Drive me crazy? *Uh-huh.*

I remember the first time. We are going to go very fast, he said, buckling me down. He sang along with Verdi and

10,000 Maniacs. His soft hair blowing, face intent, one hand cupping the smooth wooden sphere that juts rudely between his thigh and mine. Shifting gears, he talks to me, about two girls who want him at once, together: one who loves only the driving, with his cupped hand making sensitive moves between him and her; one who is barely fifteen, with pale yellow hair and astonishing legs. I listen. You, he said, not then, but at some other time, times. You, but I can't. Cahn't. Want to pick you up and take you away. And, but, of course, I cahn't. If only you were not who you are. My best friend's *mother*.

Oh, I say. Oh, *that*.

Go inside and buy some maps. Maybe an illuminated magnifier. Mark the routes, and all the stops. *Go* on. It was a command. Wait, I pleaded, don't we, don't you want to see this lovely old seaside town? Beautiful cars sliding into place? Look! A Wolseley Hornet!

We were at the starting post, beside the elegant turreted mansion, surrounded by rare and beautiful machines, Victorian follies, lawns rolling to the Irish Sea. A movie set. Don't you want . . . ? Is that a Sunbeam? Oh—

He picked me up, all slung about with heavy weights— camera, notebook, gumboots, heart. *Maps*, he said, putting me down, turning away to fool with the fuel pump. Torque wrench, I thought he said, to himself. That was in another country, I murmur. And besides, the wrench is dead.

There was an announcement. Some delay. Bomb warning; muffled telephone voice, explosives in a car. Classic car? One of us?

Maps. I begin to run, up the steps, into the airless smoky hall where a hundred and fifty serious navigators sit hunched over their lighted magnifiers, their Hopkirk Romer measuring gadgets, for use with their 1:50,000 ordnance survey maps. Inchworms, measuring the marigolds. Kilometers in tenths, stretched across great unfolded squares of sepia-toned terra incognita. Northern Ireland. Unapproved roads. They are Sellotaping the dangerous world, lest they land, by mistake, in the dark, facing a young blond English girl soldier with her M-16 rifle at the ready, shouting a command to stop, firing anyway. Questions later.

I've brought some champagne, Ludo shouted after me as I ran. In case we do well.

Mountains of Mourne, county of Down, and what do we have in Roscommon? In less than an hour, barring explosions, we are to drive off into the unmarked night, tunneling through hedgerows, everything obscured but the crossing of our stars.

Besides the champagne, I noted, he has brought boxes of music, of cigarettes, whiskey, and chocolate bars. None of these is for me. Go and chat up those two in the Berlini ti, he snapped over his shoulder. See if they'll let you copy their maps. Go *on*.

How can I? Why should they? They've spent six hours marking the route. Everyone has. Everyone but us. Sitting in that smoke, making hieroglyphs based on arcane instructions. Look at these! Ludo scowls, shakes his head. Torque wrench.

I go back to mill again in the smoke, hopelessly, among the crack drivers with names like Pluckrose, Mutch, Larkworthy, Rushforth, Shams, Playfair, Deadman.

Someone stops me. Didn't you navigate for Stopoff in the Pirelli? I'm not sure, I say, smiling. The TV camera begins to follow me with a microphone disguised as a dust mop on a spike.

Do I look as though I might say something colorful? The American companion of that brilliant, that erratic fellow in the silver. . . .

According to the telephone warning, it had been buried in shrubbery near the starting position, some distance from the hotel parking lot. A brief delay was announced while race officials and *gardai* in plain clothes made a search of the hotel grounds. Nothing was found. Scrutineering of the competing cars was not more thorough than usual, although black sensor devices passed smoothly, solemnly, across and down each vehicle, as if bestowing some ominous blessing.

There used to be thirty-nine bomb warnings in Belfast every day. Most were hoaxes, all disrupting ordinary life. Buildings evacuated, streets emptied. And once in London, British Rail got a forty-five-minute warning to empty every main-line station during the rush hour. They decided not to. That one wasn't a hoax. Can't win them all.

Ludo on the phone, twice a day. Saying, Please come, I'll pencil us in, there, between my next two big races, perfect. Wait till you see my white crash helmet. All right? We'll race the silver car. It will be perfect. Just say yes. Walking my windy beach, I imagined scenes, obscenes, staring rudely at the suggestive shapes of seaweed stalks, seeing his slow waking smile, bare arms stretched backward, framing his head like rainbows.

Then he calls suddenly, a third time, at night—he who never calls at night, never from home, never while drinking wine, while thinking of me. Wanting to talk, saying he is afraid of this, saying he knows what I feel, it is palpable, he is torn by it, by what *he* feels, which is what, again? His loyalties and urges, his fierce creed, which I do not believe for a minute, am not willing to believe, knowing only that what is palpable is also undeniable. I am too old not to respect the undeniable when it is moving over me at 130 MPH on an unapproved road. My son's best friend.

What are we to do, then, he says. Shall we tell your son, my friend, that we are having an affair? He already thinks so. It will destroy him. (I think: It will only intrigue him, as it does you. I don't say that.) If I were gay, he is saying fervently, Sam would be my lover. When I get married, he'll be my best man—

Why do you call me every day? I blurt. Stop calling me. Damn you.

Well, he says. I cahn't stop. This is—happening. I'm afraid of—I mean don't come expecting—

I won't come. At all.

But I want you to, want you here, want you.

Ah.

There's going to be tears.

He knows I am writing of him, of him and me, of cars and sex. He likes this; I knew he would. It's what I can give him, I who am not fifteen, with tawny silk hair, not a girl with a crush, or an old flame who burned for him too long, with too ferocious a hope. I do not perform with the chorus of London derrières, or the New York careerists careering wildly into his speeding distant hands. What is in me for him? You're brilliant, he says. The nineties word for swell.

I do understand. Beauty's game is danger, the tempting of fate to relieve the boredom of irresistibility. What will happen if I dare this? Nothing. This? Nothing. *This?* He says, How shall I go in wherefrom my friend came out? He says, If only you were not who you are. But, I do not reply, where then would the enchantment lie? I love you, I say instead. He says it back, or perhaps he said it first. *You* love *me*, he says. Curt. I catch my breath, sharp and fragile as glittering shards in my throat. If only . . . he goes on. Or if only . . .

Later in the night I woke thinking: I am covered with a skin of light. I shine; everyone must see it. Next day walking my lonely strand, I saw an iridescent silver fish, breathing— or gasping, it seemed—just out of the sea. And I lifted and flung it, not gently enough, not far enough, back into the black waves wherefrom it came out. Then I looked at the inside of my rescuing hand and found soft shreds of silvered rainbow clinging to my skin, palm, fingertips. Not scales, but transparent traces of color, like film, like a second skin. They hate to be touched.

I want you. . . . I do not reply to that. Do not say But then you'll be gone in your white crash helmet. I say only I'm coming. Hang the cost, all the costs. I am leaping, like my fool of a fish out of its element, leaching torn silvery rainbows upon the warm palm of his careless flinging hand.

It is almost time. They are scrutineering Lancia Aurelia and Avenger Tiger, Lagonda and Triumph Vitesse. Ludo is still scowling. I dart back for one last try into the smoke and find a navigator with a fully Sellotaped world unfolded across three tables. Pencil lines, arrows, and circles—precise enough for any spy thriller. He could be the one carrying explosives. Help, I say softly. He smiles. Avenger Tiger cheerfully marks tonight's route, with all the control stops, on my map. Should hold you till dinner, he says. I doubt it. I buy an illuminated magnifier. Also a Romer, an ordnance survey map, a Mars bar . . .

Ludo seems pleased with my seduction of Tiger. He likes the magnifier too. I feel like an unloved child, grateful for any smile at all, between slaps.

Just ahead of us, two beautiful young men in a tomato-colored Lotus are fastening their magnolia hide tonneau cover. Snap. Every last snap. I look them up in the list of entrants. Might have guessed one would be Zan Playfair, I say. Ludo is no longer favoring me with the smile. We are next for the scrutineer. This is serious. In spite of the deafening roar of Gilbert & Sullivan that he has selected for takeoff.

The TV crew races toward us, waving their fluff-covered microphones.

What's that music? What's he driving? Who is *she*? Now, he smiles. My Pied Piper.

Within three minutes we are lost. Tiger neglected to mark the way out of town.

Two and three-quarter miles, T-junction, signpost YIELD . . .

Yield? . . . I remember the first time I tried that. In Ludo's flat, it was. His tub surrounded by mirror, his kitchen by very good wine, his bed by amusing pornography. He said: I would really like to be someone's toy-boy. (But not yours, was understood.) He said: A woman at the party last night tried to recruit me for an escort service. This is her card. I said: Well, then. This was all before. This was when I still resisted knowing his game. Beauty's game, always the same. Hide-and-seek, taunt and tease. What's wrong with flirting? he said earnestly, melting-eyed, across the table. Before I could gauge the depth of the melt. Or even that it was caused by contact lenses. He wears them all the time. Beauty is not such a fool for beauty, I did at least know that. Knew why, too: Beauty must be the only one in the room. And when male, Beauty needs constant reassurance. *Tell* me I'm beautiful, he commands. Go on, make me feel the way you look at me. Not that I trust it; what if I lost everything? Face ruined, beauty smashed?

It is something to consider: How will Ludo feel, the first night he walks into a restaurant and everyone goes right on eating? Will there be life thereafter? He pleads: Would you come to see me after I crashed, after I wrecked my body? Disfigured, paralyzed? Of course, I lied. Uh-huh.

I polished the mirror surrounding his marble bath. While I'm here, I reflected, he will see himself without streaks, on any side. Perfect. I once heard him say: I like all my cars to be perfect. He said it in a rage, punching a hole in the precious, rusted silver door. His mechanic shrugged. That Ludo, he muttered, shaking his head. We all need Ludo's reflections to be perfect.

And, but, there was too much wine when we were together. Ludo put me to bed, I don't remember how. A boîte down the street, steak tartare and wine—wine before, during, instead. Then he folded out the sofa bed, folded me into it. Went inside to his amusing porn.

Once I brought him a photocopy of my novel in typescript, a thing I never do, never wanting to be read raw, like steak tartare, while I am there, by a stranger whose name I have already stolen twice for unsavory characters, not because I think him unsavory, but because it was a way of touching him, without touching him. A claim. Besides, I like his name, and his dangerous habits, looking at them, reading them, sounding them silently, in an interior voice, a voice I know only when I feel its echo in the center of my body.

He turns up the music now with the look that means I am no help. The camera crews call gaily as we pull up to the border crossing: customs halt, time control checkpoint. Louder! It's a song called "Too Fast." About sex, not cars. His music whips about us like banners. Tenth of a mile, a bridge, road veers left, take the right. Calibrations, more hieroglyphs, sheaf of mystifying charts. Not a prayer, says Ludo. Still I am no help. I'll hold the wheel, I offer hopefully. You translate the code. Somehow it begins to work, I feel his rising heat, his sudden astonished hope, and for the first time, he says, Here, you drive. The smile dawns; I have earned it; mine. Like a six-year-old who has just sold her daddy a five-cent lemonade. We trade places, I drive. Look at me, I think. I exult. The euphoria lasts nearly an hour. Signposts: GIVE WAY, WAY OUT, ignore a dirt road. Everything suggests impending doom. I speed giddily on. Trouble surrounds us, mist descending over the mountain, a green Standard or a black Rochdale Olympic, or the Morgan 4/4 tailing us too close, headbeams shedding frosted light on the steep stone flanks of invisible hillsides. If we were being polite, he says, we'd let them pass. Not being polite! I shout, jubilant. Putting my foot down.

Supposed to keep it at 30, he says, suddenly scolding. This is *calibrated*. He, who averages 120 on one-lane hairpins, accelerating at the blind crest, fiddling with his stereo, skidding. I know these roads, I say softly. Been driving this very car, on these very roads, in this very mist. Don't brake at the corner, he snaps. Accelerate at the corner. I disobey. You're doing 35, he says. Tense now. Gone, the smile. My hard-won smile. He who does 90, swerving, lighting a cigarette, taking the turn on two wheels. While I say nothing. We are almost down the mountain. There's a terrific crash, behind us, just invisible. Not hit, are we? I say. I know we are not. Ludo knows too. But he's shouting, I don't know! Jumping out, grim-faced, ashen. All I know, he yells inexplicably, is I'm getting out of this!

What have I done?

Of course we are not hit. The green Standard has crashed. Tailing us too fast, out of control, driving without brakes, not even a hand brake. They had steered deliberately into the rock face, rather than hit us at 60 MPH. Ludo takes photographs of the wreck, then climbs back into the driver's side. That's it, he says; we're finished.

What did I do? It is not discussed. Just read the directions, he says coldly, I try; signpost Burnfoot, T-junction, take a left. Not good enough, he says. Let me see it. He seizes the pages. Now he is driving and navigating, both.

Signpost: Burnfoot, T-junction, take a left; road curves STOP. He'll never trust me again. I try one last time: Two twenty-seven; ignore a right, keep straight—

What? he shouts. Give it to me again. Keep giving it to me. Can't you.

He is doing 80. It's dark now. I see nothing. The tears begin, however. My voice fails.

One twenty-four, a crossroads, road angles left. YIELD . . .

Again, he says. And the next one, keep talking. Can't you. *Cahn't* you.

No. I am finally sobbing. He is doing 110. I can't. I *cahn't*.

He exhales, grabs all the papers again.

More sobbing. What is it? he demands then. Talk to me. Can't you.

After a while I gasp: You're . . . a bully. (What I mean is, Stop the car. And hold me.)

Bully! he sneers. You think this race is some joke, some tour of the bloody Irish countryside. This is . . . I care about it. Not about winning, but— And you . . . don't care . . . at all.

This shocks me into silence. I see his head turn suddenly, at the sound of lapwings. No more of those in England, he murmurs. See how their wings go. And I weep secretly for the sweetness in him, bittered by too much easy "love." *Would* I come to see him after he crashed, wrecking his body? Of course not.

I am a rotten bastard, he says lightly. In my impeccable Prince of Wales checkered suit, my white silk dinner jacket, my outrageous black-fringed buckskin. I am a shit, but still suitable for bringing home to their parents. And they ring me up, offering their bodies two at a time. I don't play back the messages anymore.

I wince, remembering the last time I phoned him from Dublin airport. He did pick up that one. This character Ludo, I said gaily, is about to board a plane with me. We're flying to Paris. I'm writing a story about us. We're going to have a great time.

Do you end up in love with him? he asked matter-of-factly.

I start out in love with him.

Do you end up hating him, then? Is he a shit?

I didn't answer, quite. The only question, I said instead, is whether he's a terrorist.

Really? he laughed. Brilliant! Don't call him Ludo, though. Where will you be in Paris? I'll ring you.

You can't, I say. The last of my coins expires.

I'll call you, he says again. Darling?—

He and I were inventing him then. Inventing us. What fun.

I would write about the way he always speeds, parks illegally, leaves valuables gleaming on the seat, flirts with the wrong sorts of "grown-ups," a word he is quick to tell you is a child's vision of adulthood; a child's notion of simply becoming higher. It's all of a piece, the come-and-get-me, hide-and-seek, daring devils—is it devils, or merely grown-ups?—to pay attention to small, unloved Ludo. I told him I would tell of the tenderness, the boy with his head lifted, listening to lapwings, the boy who remembers Connecticut woods, geese on the pond, leaves like shards of a stained-glass window; restoring his first car, loving his first girl, and the first moment he saw his own beauty as a lethal weapon.

Promise, he said. I promised.

And don't call him Ludo.

At midnight he needs to have the car washed and polished after its first long day in the wild wet dangerous country. There is only one petrol station open for miles, and the washing machine balks at having to do laundry at this hour.

Impatient with the sleepy attendant who cannot get the thing started, Ludo grumbles: Perhaps it's true what they say about the Irish. I tell him the one about the three prisoners and the faulty guillotine. When the blade fails to drop, the condemned man goes free. First the Englishman is saved, then the Frenchman. It is the Irishman's turn. He looks up at the stuck blade and says: I think I can fix that.

Ludo is delighted; I am rewarded with his wonderful laugh, which echoes in the desolate petrol station, startling the attendant. Something clicks into place; the beautiful silver nose of our charger rises gently on its pedestal, to be showered with caresses by violent red and blue whirling mops, to be lathered and rinsed and rolled off into the chilly blue light. Ludo gazes at it emerging from its bath, as if it were Botticelli's Venus. Then he looks at me, and his eyes fill

15

with sudden reproach. I gave this to you, this beautiful thing which is God to me, and you refused it. For months! Let it sit rusting in this cold, in this damp. You chose to ride in rented plastic Japanese boxes. How could you? It's as if . . . as if you dedicated a book to me, and I kept it, unread, in a rubbish bin.

I was afraid, I say softly. Of you, of crashing—one way and another.

His eyes blaze. I would have had you crash it; I told you. Didn't you understand? Don't you, even now?

The car gleams between us in the darkness. We climb in and drive silently to the hotel. I go first; he is still with the car, murmuring to it, soothing it. I find my way quickly, shutting my door to the awkward moment. Seconds later he knocks, enters, kisses me on the mouth. Damn you, I want to say. Good night, he says, and is gone.

I have a bath, read five pages of a borrowed Galsworthy novel about the terrible comforts of social order. I lie awake listening to the others arriving two by two: Spiders, Beetles, Frogs, Tigers. I do not sleep at all; I imagine Ludo sleeping, wearing the smile. The wall between us is solid. The radio news says there is no news about the reported explosives in the classic car race. Scrutineers and *gardai*, military transports, cooperating at control checkpoints. . . .

I listened for distraction, to distraction. From the thought of his soft blowing hair and the memory of some other morning when I touched his skin, waking, and when he, waking, touched mine. I did not allow the sound to escape, the oh-help rising in my throat, did not murmur when he drew my head down and kissed me, brushing the skin of my thigh with a passing hand, as though it had been there before, belonged there, as though it meant no more than an ordinary hello.

From the window of the room now I see him in the predawn light, performing gentle mysterious acts inside the car, rituals of the penetralia, clearing away the evidence of our past. As I snap my camera shutter I suspect this photograph will not survive the journey. Like the ones he took of me last night, standing beneath the sudden, stark white road sign we passed, lost in the midnight rain, only our magnified light shining upon the arrow that warned: Unapproved Road. Exposed, he said, grinning, shrugging, arms full of black celluloid loops, like some mischievous Laocoön. Exposed.

Never find this road again, or that sign, I murmured.

Somewhere in Ireland, he replied, laughing.

In the morning I knock at his door.

Ludo in white, a towel tucked at the waist. He walks about, without even the silk robe, now that he knows, or dismisses, or counts on . . . my reaction. Perhaps he imagines that I will stumble forward, moaning, to touch him, so that he can remove my hand, before it fuses with his skin. The game of it intensifies, if only I will go on playing. But now it is I who can't. Look away, I command myself. He crosses the room again, and yet again, as if to follow my fleeing eyes.

Then he ducks into the bathroom, turns on water taps, calls out briskly:

Go study maps. See you at breakfast.

There's a bouquet in the hall outside the opposite door; I steal a white carnation and lay it across his doorknob. Signifying what? No matter. He wears it to breakfast, and all that day. The TV crew loves it. Nice touch, they say.

He smiles his smile. Cameras follow us.

Weren't you, a reporter asks me, driving the Morgan three-wheeler at Vltava?

Um, I say, not this year.

Other drivers are looking nervous. It is no longer simply a bomb threat, a device among us planted by invisible distant forces. One of these drivers is speeding it to its destination. T-junction, farmhouse on the right, ignore a dirt path, road veers. Take a left . . . One of us.

He smiles above my white carnation, at the control stop. The cameramen arrive. Nice touch, they say again, aiming the camera at the flower. He beams; he swells with unseemly pride. The mop-headed microphone nods at him. We're hopeless, he grins, you'll never see us again.

We climb back in, he turns up the stereo. Suzanne Vega croons the misty hills: *Da-do-do, da-do-do*. He's feeling better. I'm feeling worse. We get lost. The car voices objections. Fuel line blocked. At the lunch stop he says, Get some food, anything. And races off to find a petrol station. We lose time. The rain is pelting now, we are soaked, but the top stays down. Matter of pride. After a certain point, he tells the TV crew, You're as wet as you're going to be. With the game grin he turns on for them, becoming clear that he is, we are, the running gag, the comic relief of this film. His test scores are as bad as they can be. Judges mark our card "Max Penalty."

I start calling him that. He laughs. I will do anything for his laugh. TV cameramen zero in, delighted. Shots of our drenched clothes, Ludo's glorious sopping smile, his hair jeweled with raindrops.

In the mountains, I unwrap the awful official sandwiches, plus remnants of last night's supper; bits of steak and half a bottle of fair Bordeaux. We also have a new bottle of better stuff. We'll drink the better stuff first, he says. After that, the other won't taste as bad as it is. The sun comes out; warm, golden gorse surrounding us, lighting the stony flanks of Irish mountains. We are lost, as usual; tired, perversely happy. The wet silver car gleams in the road like a knight errant. Music fills the blue air:

Too fast. Oh-uh-oh . . . And he smiles over the rim of his glass, saying, Look: We have steak and wine, music and sunshine, each other. It's beautiful. What a place to—if only—

I aim my camera at him. Afraid of the end of that sweet, false sentence. He poses leaning on the car's hood, with his melt-in-your-mouth look, draining the last of the good wine.

The other bottle has been left too long in the sun. Still, nothing ventured . . . He pulls the cork, refills both glasses. Awful stuff. Neither of us quite drunk enough not to notice. Here, I say. Take a sip, then give it to me. Perhaps we can improve it.

He sips, grimaces, gulps. I say: No—I meant—

He nods primly. I know, he says. I cahn't.

Cahn't, I echo. Draining my glass quickly, in silence. Sober as a scrutineer. Swallowing pride, tears, hemlock. The taste lingers. I taste it still. I see him gazing in his mirrors, turning his body, touching his hair. Did Narcissus truly love what he saw, what he plunged to his death for? Ludo shrugs. Come on, he says. In seconds we are doing 120, plummeting down some corkscrew hill. Jesus! he yells. Don't you love this? I stare at his ecstatic face. Narcissus' mad flight from his destiny. And I get to tag along.

Each time we start, he straps and buckles me, his hands swift, impersonal.

I am held tight, prisoned, moving with him in the speeding rhythmic air, watching his hands and his mouth, his body tensing, his tender skillful parody of an act of love with the chosen partner.

I will get you, one way or another, I tease. I taunt. In print, I say. Brave threats. Am I evil? he muses, studying his profile in my eyes.

You are Lulu in *Pandora's Box*, I say. The world crashes in love with Lulu, I explain. While she streaks past, heedless, all unknowing.

Better than knowing, he says. I am not at all sure. Besides, after a while, innocence expires, like a learner's permit. At thirty, for example, when one has begun to condition the hair with henna highlights, wear silk boxer shorts, get the teeth capped; fit one's own most beautiful twenty-two-year-old face into a pale silk easel frame, for the record.

We reach the border crossing, thick with armored police cars, soldiers casting baleful red glares. Body checks, this time. Everyone out, car papers, passports.

Any news? I whisper. The blond girl soldier frisking us does not reply.

In Ludo's wallet, I spot a photograph: girl in combat boots and polka-dotted mini, leaning too far forward, thrusting her gaze at you, like a serious foundling.

"Love, V.," scrawled on the bottom. She is quite lovely, but the carefully composed hoyden is no longer irresistible. A shade past twenty-five, nowadays, is a delicate moment, even for a princess. Especially for a princess still reconciling freckles, baby fat, bare knees, fresh mouth, boring official duties. Her Royal Highness the Princess Victoria Anne.

We are being scrutineered for real, this time. I whisper, Why won't they call off the rally?

They think they can handle it, Ludo whispers back. Now that they know it's not on a timer.

Who told them? How do *you* know?

His sigh is exasperated, as though he's got to keep demonstrating shoelace-tying to a slow three-year-old.

Everyone's been told, he says. At the last checkpoint. There was an official decision to go on. For morale, for international publicity. There's no danger to the participants, or the public.

How—how come?

The device, the stuff, whatever it is, someone is just transporting it. It's meant for—well, it's not something that will just go off.

Not even if he crashes?

Not even.

Ludo? I catch hold of his wet sleeve.

Get in the car. It's raining.

I laugh, in spite of him. Of everything. Please, I say, though.

He shrugs me off, frowning.

At the rest stop, rumors fly. Did you know Princess Victoria is in this race? Using an alias, but everyone seems to know. What's she driving? Don't know. There are four all-woman teams, dozens of female co-drivers. Wives. Girlfriends. Me.

I peer closely at the all-woman teams. Scruffy cheap lot, nylon parkas and woolly hats, cars all N.I. license plates. If she's here, she must be co-driving with some hotshot in a red Lotus. I look hard for the famous mane of honey-blond hair. She wouldn't be flaunting it.

If it's true, Vicky is racing without official blessing. Her minders would have said no, or spoiled the fun with security hysteria. Someone, however, knows.

So, how much do they pay you? I ask Ludo lightly.

Pay? he laughs. I am strictly amateur. Love of the sport. Although I do get sponsored once in a while. He tosses me a reproachful glance, the kind a puppy gives you when he's guilty, but knows you haven't the heart to prosecute.

Sponsored. By paramilitary terrorists, for instance?

Car companies. People who make tires.

So you race for them, that's all?

Wear their name over my heart. On my car. On my lips if I'm on TV.

That's all?

No answer. Read me the map, will you? I think we're lost again.

I read him the map. How do they find you—these sponsors?

Oh, contacts. Like anything else.

Darling, he says, at the lunch stop. Get some food, I don't care what, I've got to find . . . a garage, bloody fuel line's clogged again. I need—

Torque wrench, I say, forcing a smile.

He looks at me sharply. Lack of respect. Twenty lashes. Max penalty.

The pub is a zoo, two hundred scruffy drinkers battling over three trays of dry sandwiches, cookies, and a coffee urn. Ludo will kill me if I don't get him something. Smile at that: Ludo will kill me. I grab with fists, like the rest. They're beginning to file out now; motors revving. Scan the crowd; look for tendrils of red-gold hair escaping from a woolly hat. She'd have dyed it, or worn a wig. Or would she? This girl is a daredevil, she half wants to be recognized, wouldn't I?

I am remembering photographs of her in the royal gossip rags. The prancing princess, wiggling it in jeans, bikinis. Modeling undies, they censored that one. Royal knickers. Why not? Dancing with a Black rock star. Going down in a balloon.

A couple of girls are kicking their car, giggling. It's broken down so many times. One dives underneath, cursing. Bloody hell! Northern accent. Northern slang. That unmistakable rise at the end of the sentence.

Needle in a haystack? Not for Ludo. And where's he gone to? Find a garage—report to his superiors? Torque wrench. I wander, peering vaguely at every female face. Then it strikes me—she's entered as a male. National Velvet. Liz Taylor gets Mickey Rooney to chop off her curls, and she's off, prepubertal girl jockey in her racing silks, riding her horse to win. Why not? Proportion of male to female rally drivers, even co-drivers, is what? twenty to one, fifty to one? Maybe she races all the time, without anyone blowing her cover.

I hear the deafening roar of Ludo coming; half a mile off; doing 90. Drivers exchanging sly smiles, TV crew jerking their heads, trying to catch the music. It's just some girl screaming about her lover's fear of silence.

He charges in, skidding on two wheels. Come on, he yells, we've lost five minutes. I climb in, with his lunch. All fixed? I say, trying to sound natural. He shakes his head, no, reaches out a hand. I put a sandwich in it.

I take it we are not talking. Give me directions, will you, he says.

I begin my recitation: 2.2 miles signpost Larne . . . Sheep-dog trials, I say.

What?

Sheep—it's where they—in Larne—

What?

Road curves left, stay straight, I say, chastened. Tears spring into place, I feel them. Right at home. The sky blurs; stinging wind from the sea. Not a day for the incomparable Fair Head, for the shimmer of Scotland just across, one could almost swim to it. Ludo, I don't say, please stop, I need to show you something . . . beautiful. I swallow the ache, remembering the sweet turn of his head, listening to the lapwings. But that was yesterday.

Where does Ludo go when he disappears? Youth wants to know.

I told you. The fuel line was clogged. It's still clogged.

So where did you go?

Some idiot garage. Two garages. We're still losing power.

So is America. They're pissed, also. Enough to kill people. Which reminds me, have you spotted your princess?

My—?

I must say it was gratifying. That look. Guilt, amazement, and the sort of startled pleasure a teacher displays when the slowest pupil suddenly catches on. Ludo's smile, Ludo's laugh, was worth anything. Well, almost.

Princess, I said. Her Royal Highness Vicky Anne.

Who told you *that*? he snapped.

Little bird. Lapwing. Goose. You're not going to insult me now, are you? Not going to say I'm crazy, wrong, stupid, hysterical? Surely . . .

I could see at least three warring factions at work in his beautiful jaw: pride, pride, pride.

Oh, double oh seven, I sighed, nobody does it better.

The car veered so sharply I thought he'd lost control. All *right*, he said. Cold as black ice. We were in a ditch, in a fog, on an unapproved road. Get out, then. Come on. Well? I didn't move. Except for my heart and mind, the flow of my blood, the lurch of my sexual being.

No sir, I cried. Can't, won't. Not like this, not on your life. That was funny. But his smile was gone.

All right, then, he leered like some stage villain. Don't let it be said—

Little Ludo couldn't carry his load—

What's that?

A song, I said. About being loaded. And needing one more. For the road.

He was back in his seat, strapped, speeding, impassive. Listen, he said, I'm sorry. I'm very sorry. He sounded so sincere.

That tears it, I said. Ludo darling.

Border crossing.

I'm not here to kill any princesses, he said. Just so you know.

Uh-huh. Friends, however? Co-drivers? Me?

I *said* I was sorry.

You didn't say what for, though. I assumed all you meant was sorry for me.

Would you mind, he said gently, reading the map?

Are you going to blow us all up? Are you? Are you?

In my own ears it was the wail of a bored five-year-old on the trip to Grand Canyon. Are we there, yet? Daddy, Daddy. Are we there yet?

Did you volunteer, or did they find you? Originally, I mean. The first time.

This is the first time, he said, swerving so suddenly I screamed.

Dogs, he said. Damned Irish dogs, think it's the national sport. Running under wheels.

Well, I murmured, perhaps they too want not to die of boredom. Better at high speed; die while you're still drop-dead gorgeous. All the world mourns Dudley, his brave little heart crushed under a careless silver Alfa Romeo.

He lurched to a stop. Come on, then, he said, jumping out, standing beside me, yanking the door open. Losing time, I said.

I'll make it up.

I'm sure you will.

So?

Ludo, stop. You don't really want this.

How could I not? How?

His eyes were unnaturally bright, feverish. No fair, I thought. No fair fighting myself over him; whatever I do he wins. Killer take all. Nevertheless when he bent to unbuckle me I put my hand on his neck, the hand he had once so righteously, so forcibly, removed from that very, that very soft, spot. It is as I remembered. A moan escapes me; I would give something to get it back. His face is surrounded by sudden sun, as though flames leak from its edges. All right, then, I thought, falling toward it, into it, other people have died of this. He lifted me out of the car, gently. I am light, weightless, like a movie heroine perishing of TB, or some mysterious poison. Dressed in gossamer panels fluttering like a shroud. It's raining again, I notice. The ground is already wet, the air fragrant.

I begin to swim toward him as though my life depended on it, as though my arms were lifting from the sea, trailing phosphorescent wings. Help, I said. I cahn't, he said. Those were all the words.

After a while I take his wrist in my hand, and press it, the blue-veined inside of it, to my mouth. What? he said. My wrist? I shook my head. Time to go, I say. Follow that car, driver. He checks the nature of my smile, nods. We are both drenched, but I am pouring, like the elements. I cannot tell where they end and I begin.

We are doing 130 before I say anything. And what I say is: You're in love with this princess? Is that why?

My God, what a question.

But you won't answer it.

Not in love with "this princess." How's that?

Were you ever? *Any* princess?

Darling, I hate all princesses. By definition.

Odi et amo. I hate and I love. Catullus. My teeth are chattering.

Drink this. He unscrews the cap of his silver flask. Whiskey. I hate whiskey. I gulp it down. Hold tight, now. We're going to make up for lost time.

Lost time. Perfect. We were cresting a steep hill. Signpost: Dangerous Bends, Test Your Brakes! Ludo laughed. Never use brakes. Wears them out. Show you how to take these corners—like Nuvolari, when he took the German Grand Prix away from Hitler, 1935—

Oh God—look out!

Two cars dead in the road, smoking. Ludo shrieks to a stop. It's the Lagonda! he yells. Christ . . .

Anyone hurt? Dazed fellows milling about in the fog. Surrounded by locals, farmers, cows, sheepdogs, horse carts, and tractors. Ludo the Samaritan says: What can I do to help?

Nothing. Notify the sweepers. Ashen, the drivers stand beside the corpses of their loved ones. A million pounds to resurrect that, Ludo says. How did it happen? Black ice, back there—we barely missed it. Car starts dancing on that, you've bought it. Million pounds' worth.

Well, winter's coming, I say. They'll be driving their closed cars till spring, anyway.

He gives me a killer look. I deserve it; not respectful.

Hard to believe that half an hour ago that mouth was soft, his wet hair streaming across my breast.

I am shivering. Want the top up? he says. I shake my head. Let's go, then.

The maps are so wet it doesn't matter whether I cry or not. Three point two miles, a bridge, house on the right, take a left . . .

He flicks on the stereo. Want to drive? he says. He looks at me. I don't answer, just keep my eyes on the map.

I said do you want—

I heard you. No.

Right. He accelerates. 100, 110. The road is slick—like a bottle, the Irish say. 120. I close my eyes.

What's she like? The—Victoria Anne.

Like a princess.

In a fairy tale?

In an anachronism. Empty symbol of privilege and lost power; a waste product.

What's it to you, though?

It's nothing to me.

Since when is murder nothing?

No such thing as murder anymore. There's only peripheral damage.

Servicing the target, I murmured. When the lethal gas is piped into the front of the truck full of Jews and Gypsies, there's a tendency for "the load" to shift to the rear. Requiring adjustments of the chassis design, to take that into account.

Women! Ludo sighed; the needle hit 130.

There was an abnormally large crowd lining the road at the next time-control checkpoint. Considering the weather, the time of night, and the location. Middle of nowhere. Two point three miles from the middle of nowhere. Then we spotted the armored vehicles, drivers out of cars, grim-faced rally officials.

Another bomb warning. Ludo, expressionless, sprang out, opened my door like some gallant junior prom escort. Soldiers surrounded the car, aiming black boxes at it like accusing fingers. No, like video remote-control zappers, desperately scanning channels. Then they did us. Papers, pockets, luggage, faces. Tense nods. We drive on.

The rough-voiced Belfast girls pass us. Their ancient Reliant rattles like a Halloween skeleton, stalling out on hills, crying for radiator water, or a bullet to its head. The girls are all bluster and hard cheer; you can imagine them in their local pub, scuffed cowboy boots up on the rail. One has purple spikes for hair; the other, younger, has a wedding ring and a gap-toothed grin. Ludo keeps stopping to chat, offer help, trade war stories. There they are again, he says happily; he loves it that they're game losers, won't quit. In Monte Carlo last year, they tell us, they pushed the car for the cliff-hanging last mile, to finish the race. Well, I've got my favorites too: Zan and Giles, in their tomato red Lotus, who will, even in lashing rain, snap their magnolia leather tonneau cover on and off as though this were a military drill. I eavesdrop on them shamelessly. Giles is forty-odd, running (or driving) to soft fat. Zan is blond, hard-boiled, dazzling-toothed—the teeth of a boy guide at Disney World. Giles calls him "dear boy." Anyone would. He tosses his hair like a pony.

All the same, they're doing brilliantly, especially Zan in the tests—never makes a mistake. And on the road, smooth as silk. You'd think they were on automatic pilot.

Zan eyes Ludo from time to time. Cruising him? In the pub, at the test sites, I see, think I see, that coded flicker, flashing silent signals. Are you one? Just this once? Where would that leave Giles? Let alone me. Don't they ever care?

I check Ludo's expression. He seems never to notice Zan at all. In fact, his not noticing seems exaggerated. That Ludo doth protest too much, I say, to amuse myself. Gallows humor.

Could Victoria Anne be one of those Belfast chickies, in that hopeless wreck of a car? Would that be royal fun? I have to guess not. Ludo's attentions notwithstanding. Well, how about that very pretty co-driver in the TR-6; more her speed?

Princess Victoria has always been a royal pain in the ass. Remember that news photograph of her, age three, scowling furiously at the camera, while her serene elder brother favors the world with a vague little smile destined to rule for sixty years. Even if—especially if—there's nothing left to rule.

Victoria Anne had no smile, then or now. Only that defiant baby fist of a face.

Just ahead of us, a sign warned: Dangerous Bridge. One of those ancient right-angle, blind-entry stone bridges. Specialty of the Irish landscape. Two Minis lined up behind a lorry. Ludo peeled the wrapper off a candy bar. The explosion was so loud, in that perfect stillness, that for a minute all my senses denied it. See no evil, hear no evil. Ludo still clutching the candy bar, his fingers closed over it; chocolate fist. The car trembled for its life. The bridge was gone, leaving the front end of the lorry dangling over water like a reticulated Dinky toy. Both Minis had overturned. Drivers and navigators crawling out. The lorry driver, miraculously unhurt, thrown clear of his truck, screaming prayers and curses into the smoldering darkness.

The rally would surely be stopped now. Princess Vicky saved. There was a meeting. Ulster TV crew invited. Officials on mobile telephones to Belfast, London. Emergency road crews, local police summoned, detour signs, arrangements.

Eighty-six rally cars had already passed this control point. No way to stop them all before night halt, hours away, miles of darkness. In half an hour the decision was reached: the race would go on.

A speech is made by the clerk of the course, another by the president of the club, still another by the chief constable. Any participant who wishes to withdraw will be listed as a finisher; B&B provided by the club, no questions asked. And anyone who leaves will be eliminated as a suspect? Well, not quite. We will ask them to sign papers. Routine, just so we'll know who and where they are. Eighteen cars withdrew. Thirty-six persons, twenty-two of them club members in good (paid-up £5 dues) standing. Elderly couple from Ban-

gor, in the Riley. She in tears. Father-and-son team from An-
glesey, England, in the red Lancia. Already sustained front-
end damage on that last set of dangerous bends. The father
had a pacemaker in his heart. The son couldn't let him go
on. I watched them all go, silent and shaken, the lot of them,
in their bright nylon parkas. I put a line through the car
numbers on the master list of entries, in my navigator's kit.
By the time the last of them had turned tail, the rally orga-
nizers had bent the rules for the rest of us, a hundred and
twenty-eight cars in all, needing new routes from here to the
night halt, fifteen miles on.

In the agonizing hours it all took, Ludo never glanced at
me. To everyone else—rally officials, fellow drivers, police,
press—he was the spirit of the event, incarnate. Helpful, car-
ing, tireless. Offering mechanical assistance, food, whiskey,
cigarettes, jokes. He was, he seemed, someone else. Ludo of
the lapwings.

I began to doubt what I knew or thought I knew, most
surely: This animal is dangerous.

Was the princess with us? Or had she crossed that bridge
before we came to it? Could she be among the eighteen
withdrawing teams? I doubted that. Headstrong, spoiled little girl, with nothing to lose but a silly, pampered life? How
much did a princess value life, anyway? Ludo would tell
you to the penny how much it cost the Brits to keep her in
champagne and off-the-face blue hats.

Eighty-six cars ahead of us, forty-two with us. Ludo still
boosting morale, gathering character witnesses. Such a nice,
good-looking boy. He reappeared, finally.

Did you know about that bridge?

His eyes were soft. How could you think that and still be in this car with me?

Where else could I be? I said. What if you really are a killer? Why would you want me here? What if— No. You couldn't. But what if you could? Finally I blurt it: Why do I suddenly think that Sam, your friend, my son, might be in New York right now, with some pal of yours in a ski mask, some pal with a gun, waiting for your phone call from some garage? Torque wrench, you could say, and—

Mm, he said. Not a bit shocked. A little smile, in fact. Well, he went on. If I told you not to worry about Sam, you're free to go with any of our thirty-six deserters, I'll get you a ride—

I wouldn't, I said.

Believe me?

Go.

He leaned over and brushed my wet forehead with his warm mouth. And I didn't cry. You're the one, I blurted instead. Aren't you? Of course you are.

No, he snapped. Wish I were, though. Brilliant. A royal assassin! Brilliant! He put on some speed, took the right-angle turn skidding. He likes to do that. Also to steer with his knees. Look, Ma, no hands.

They seek him here, they seek him there . . . I chant. Is he in heaven, is he in hell, that damned elusive—Pimpernel.

He turns up the stereo: *Baby, you can drive my car . . .*

He favors me with a smile. I read it and, now, I weep.

He reaches across me and changes the tape. It's Sam's voice. Sam! Singing his favorite sad song, "Streets of

Laredo." Dying cowboy who placed all his trust in the woman who killed him.

I scream. No. Please, no. Why did you pick me? Or was it Sam you picked?

Come on, all I did was invite you. You were dying to come.

Not quite. Dying! Am I a hostage, then? Am I? And whose side are you on, anyway? It's not even your country! Who pays you?

Everybody pays me. I'm neutral. Which is why, it's why I'm useful.

Double agent? Mercenary?

He laughed. Free agent. Entrepreneur.

Would you, oh God, at least tell me where Sam is? How could you involve Sam?

I told you he's all right. Want to call him?

Is—someone there with him? In his apartment?

Probably find him watching *Law and Order* with a friend or two.

Friend—who? One of your— Does he know about you? Of course not. How could he? Is it a friend with a gun?

Get a grip, Ludo said. It was—a bad joke. *Law and Order.* Come on, lighten up. We'll call him from the night stop. Okay?

Straight answer! Just one. Oh, please, you *bastard*.

Thought you. Thought I was swell.

My God, you made sure of that too! Part of the plan.

He reached over suddenly, rumpled my hair.

My mind, racing the speedometer. On the stereo, Sam is

still singing. Songs of death, abandonment, fear, imprison-
ment, despair. Songs about train wrecks, destruction, loss.

But that's just Sam, I think. Ludo too. Isn't it? That's just
all of them, in love with themselves as doomed James Dean,
Marilyn, Lawrence of Arabia. Ludo is watching my eyes; I
empty them. He switches the tape. Something about a girl
having fun fun fun, till her daddy takes the T-bird away.

Ludo? What would a boy like you be doing in a plot like
this?

Plot like what?

Bomb plot. A bomb of a plot.

He laughs. If we finish, and don't come in last, it won't be.

Why does his light tone so not comfort me? Gasping, I
study his profile. He is intent now on the acutely bending
road. His mouth softening in that way it does, moving
downward into a child's pout, all lower lip, all hurt and disappointment. Border crossing, I manage to say. Crisp, neutral. But I look at him meaningfully. Is it in this car? Is it?
Why? Why?

Stop it, he says, pulling smoothly into line for the next test.
Get a grip, he says.

It's raining again, hard. Last year Ludo won a champagne
bet driving from Oslo to Monaco without once putting the
top up. Blizzard, hailstorms. Want the top up? he says. I
shake my head, brave little soldier.

And then I remember: Princess! What does she really look
like, apart from the famous flaming hair? I realize I can't
imagine. Men—and the media—seem to fixate on the hair.
Then, if there's nothing seriously amiss (glasses, big nose),

they check size of breasts, shape of legs, ass, how tall she is in relation to them. These are the approved visual targets; more important, these are quantifiable. Which is why the face of a female criminal or victim or celebrity is so easy, so impossible, to describe. The media does "blond bombshell," "smoldering brunette." In the old days fat was "Junoesque"; scrawny was "willowy"; ugly was "striking." In the press, every violently killed woman under forty is always beautiful, like every bride.

Victoria Anne. The photo in Ludo's wallet. In her official portraits the line from bosom to waist is long, tapered, elegant. The tabloids used to give us blurred action shots; a redhead, round, running. Little Vicky. Then, after she lost weight, she became the titian-haired tomboy. Royal rebel without a cause.

Each royal generation badly needs its daredevil. This redhead, flaming torch, sporting hot pants, her tiara at a rakish angle, going 150 miles an hour to her destiny. The world wags its stern finger, TV shakes its fond head. That Vicky. That princess.

Ludo, I said, what if you can't spot her for sure? I mean, what will you blow up then? All of us?

We'll find something, he snapped.

That bridge doesn't count?

Did I blow up a bridge?

We are both crazy. I suddenly think: The next time he changes the tape, or lights a cigarette, I could seize the wheel and crash us into some ancient crumbling wall. With my luck, my navigating, we'd be only horribly crippled. And they could kill Sam, anyway. Or if they didn't, he'd have to take care of—I almost said "us"—for life. And all I'd save would be some bored little brat with too many diamonds. Not fair. Don't even know the girl. Maybe she's destined to save rain forests. Or discover the cure for upper-class wife beating. She could grow up to be La Pasionaria, give her entire dress allowance to the Society for Sick and Indigent Room-keepers. Who am I not to save *her*?

Ludo is still watching me. Guinea for your thoughts, he says. Sterling.

I force a smile. Five quid, I say. Cost of living's just gone up.

News on the car radio, it's two A.M.: In Northern Ireland today, the historic Circuit of Ireland retrospective car rally, beset by troubles since its start in Belfast forty-eight hours ago . . . Tonight in . . . a bridge blown up. Extremist paramilitary group claimed responsibility, a telephoned warning fifteen minutes before the explosion. An escort of British army helicopters is now following the rally cars, as they speed along an undisclosed detour route through the darkness. In an unrelated accident, two participating cars met disaster near Armagh city—one driver injured . . .

Ludo snapped it off.

Don't you want to know if it was the princess?

I know it wasn't.

How?

Trust me.

Oh, I do. I do.

Night sky, slippery pearl road, like driving inside the

shell of a Galway oyster. He's playing "Fast Car" again. About driving fast enough to get high, to be someone. Else. . . .

Clots of children from scattered bungalows gather along the ghostly hedgerows, screaming with delight as the cars streak past. We are shiny, dangerous aliens from some other planet. Ludo has scrapbooks full of pictures like this, from third world countries where he races. Grinning urchins lining the route; beauty queens posing on the car bonnets, sashes and garlands draped over the passing heroes. Heroes! In all these photographs, Ludo wears a sheepish grin. Apologetic. God forgive me, I love this so. Lawrence of Arabia surrounded by dark adoring girls or boys, any one of whom, *oh* yes, behind the dunes, quick!

But he's not, Ludo is no Lawrence. True passion—love or madness—is missing. Baroness Orczy's Scarlet Pimpernel risked his neck to save undeserving aristos. A hero who loved his class, and the system, however rotten. A proper daredevil for a baroness. For peasants, Robin Hood is more like it. Ludo is no Robin either. No Hemingway freedom fighter, no cool bounty hunter. Ludo is nothing but a road warrior. Ludo *is* his car.

At last we find the control stop, *garda* checkpoint. Soaked and shivering, needing the hot baths, the champagne, dry clothes, supper, night halt. I, needing something more, or something else, drank enough to miss the verb, if there was a verb, and the point, if there was a point, of the only sentence I remember. Like a shot, Ludo whispered, looking at me like an unrequited lover. If only you were not . . . Oh, I got that, heard that echo clearly, felt it pierce certain interior tissues, leaving a sweet ache I thought I recognized.

In the hotel lounge bar, drivers are milling with locals, tourists. Lady in green Indian silks, with bells on. Moving to music, fluttering her panels. Limp, they were. She was. And the younger ones, mostly in black, displaying their last legs, midriffs, at thirty, thirty-two, who'll buy? Not Ludo. He will, however, buy the party. Sumptuous. Money and boredom. He talks to a tall blond Nazi-haircut girl in severe black lapels. Spangled hot pants move across his field of vision. He fills his glass, plate, eyes. Exchanges business cards and telephone numbers. A film producer; a banker; Zan Playfair. Spangled hot pants announces, tightly, It's my birthday and I'm very drunk, and if you're not, go away. She flashes the skin that was hidden beneath her black jacket. A spangled bustier carefully saved for this moment. Ludo isn't looking. He's seen it.

Bedtime, he says to me. Waiting for the elevator, I say, How sad they all seem.

Sadder than us? he says.

Much, I say, with some heat. They have no passion at all.

He shrugs.

Don't understand you, I murmur.

Good, he says, flashing a smile. The less you know, the safer you feel. *God* knows. That's enough for most people.

For Catholics, I say.

How about Muslims? Cultists?

Psychopaths—?

He shrugs again. Every war's a holy war. Or you can't get stupid people to die for it.

Only smart people? Like you?

He sighs. I'm not fighting anybody's war, he says. Except mine.

We're walking down the corridor.

I say lightly: Yours? In aid of what? Against what?

Systems, he replies, gesturing vaguely. They've all gone rotten. All that's left is the skin of lies. In Russia, with only one TV station, one *Pravda*, people knew they were being lied to.

I nod. In the U.S., with a hundred media voices, you think someone must be telling the truth.

Right, he says. You do get it.

I shake my head. Killing as a solution? Killing some *princess*? Who decides *that*?

Night halt, he says, kissing me. We'll call Sam tomorrow.

Ludo, I plead, holding his heart against me. Tell me one thing that's true.

You love me, he says, and lets go.

I hear his door close. I could call Sam now. Or the *gardai*. Not from the room. Police call box just beyond the parking lot. Set into a crumbling stone wall, like a safe.

Sam first. Ordinary phone box at the corner. Collect. Message machine. No one can take your call right now . . .

It's ten o'clock in New York. Do you know where your children are?

There may be no police station for miles, and one patrol car to chase all the drunk drivers in the county. But the police box—called "green man"—works all night. As I run, I rehearse: Hello, I think there's a bomb in my, uh, friend's car. Who is this, where are you, what makes you think so? And the minute they show up, Ludo sends a signal to New York.

41

I stand there awhile, in the rain. Then I walk slowly back to the hotel.

At five A.M. I dress and run out to the car. Open the trunk, the hood. Stick my head in. If I trigger something, it could go off. Killing only me. And maybe Sam, five thousand miles away? I can't think of that. Standing there, looking for what? An ordinary bomb? A big bullet with tail fins, like a fifties Chevy, the sort you see in movies, raining down from U.S. planes on enemy cities. Servicing the target. Or the ones in cartoons? Round, black. A bowling ball with a smoking wick, TNT on the side in big white letters. Must be disguised as a piston. Radiator cap. Part of a stainless exhaust system. . . . Somewhere I had heard of lunchbox bombs. I imagined kids' lunchboxes, Captain Kirk, Scotty, Mr. Spock. Or Road Runner. Third-graders carrying gunpowder sandwiches in little Ziploc bags. I hook my finger through the loop of the oil stick. Check the oil? Could use a pint.

Lose something? Ludo.

I was just—

He picked me up, put me down, none too gently. I slammed the lid.

Walking back inside, he held my arm. Do that again, he said, you could cause trouble.

With the car? Or—

He pushed open my door, kissed me hard, openmouthed, tongue slipping gently in. Then: *Sleep*, he said, walking away. Damn you.

You said we could call Sam.

Morning, he said. First thing. Promise.

Morning here will be too late there—*Ludo*!

He's gone.

Sick with panic and last night's wine, sleepless, beyond tears. I cannot bear it, the lying there. I rise and stumble into the lav, whose floor space will accommodate me only in a V, jackknifed around the bowl. It is exactly what I need. I lock the door and carefully descend. Minutes pass, and suddenly he is there, outside, shouting: Open the door, what have you taken? Open it or I'll break it down!

What? I stammer. Leave me alone.

The pills! he yells.

What pills? Leave me—

I'll break it down!

I open the door and brush past him, dignified, furious. He thinks that I—he wants to think that I—God, what must his beauty lead people to do? Never mind, I can sleep now.

In the morning I find a plastic bottle of yellow pills, unmarked, not mine, inside my toilet kit. Did Ludo put it there? I do not ask. No further reference will be made to this episode.

T W O

The answering machine picks up, delivers Sam's usual teasing voice: . . . make me an offer; I might get back to you. Later, much.

It's Enjoy Ocasio, says the caller. And I do mean Enjoy. She laughs, a musical interlude. Then she adds: Or else.

The tape switches off. Sam flicks it back on and listens again, to her laugh floating in the darkness.

From his fifth-story window, if he sits at a certain angle, he can just see the point of the Chrysler building piercing the midnight sky like some moonstone deco stickpin, or the hood ornament of a classic car. Ludo would know the marque. Ludo was somewhere in Northern Ireland, doing 120 MPH with Sam's mother strapped to his passenger's seat. Sam has been trying not to think about it.

He takes a long drag and passes the smoke back to Hernando, who doesn't look any different tonight, except for the shoulder holster. If you saw him at the Time Café, or in the lobby bar of the Angelika, waiting for a decaf cappuccino, you'd assume the holster was merely a fashion statement, scarcely more eye-catching than, say, the stiletto-pointed black leather bra with metal nipples swiveling on the next bar stool. Hernando's "bra" was of course equipped with a sleek professional weapon. But you might say the other was too.

Hernando passed the joint back. He muttered something—Good shit, or I gotta shoot you. But Zulu warriors were massacring heroic Brits on the VCR, so Sam didn't quite catch it. Why, though? he said, in case the message had been relevant.

Hernando shrugged and dropped his head back against Sam's orange foldout sofa. Their colors clashed.

The phone rang again. While Sam's voice played its light-hearted tune, Hernando leapt up and began rummaging in Sam's bedroom closet. He seemed to recall a lemon-colored silk shirt.

The caller was Ludo. Hello all, he said. She loves me. He clicked off. Hernando emerged in the yellow shirt. Sam closed his eyes.

Enjoy should be here soon, Hernando announced.

Here with you, or here with me? Sam inquired politely. Not that it mattered.

Hernando giggled. He adjusted the shoulder holster, tightening the strap across his silken chest. The color scheme—yellow, orange, and Hernando—seemed more harmonious.

Are the same guys paying all of you? Or is the deal just you and Ludo?

Mango ice cream, said Hernando dreamily. Or maybe pistachio.

Fresh out, said Sam.

So call the deli.

They won't deliver after twelve.

Call Enjoy, then.

Sam dialed. Mango ice cream, he said. Help.

Hernando hit him with the butt of his gun. Blood trickled from Sam's mouth. They stared at each other in astonishment. Hernando began to sob. The devil made me do it, he said, using a silk sleeve to wipe the gun.

How much, said Sam. His voice was thick; one tooth seemed to be hanging by a thread of flesh; he could detach it with his tongue, if his tongue worked.

Not enough, said Hernando. The yellow shirt billowed with his sobbing; the holster slid up and down as if it were being jerked from behind by an unseen puppeteer.

Sam slumped forward; as he fell, Hernando jerked his foot out of the way. The door buzzer uttered its unpleasant shriek. Hernando jumped to attention. His hand shook as he held the button long enough to let Enjoy through three downstairs doors.

What if it's a burglar? The words tumbled crazily through his swollen mouth.

But Sam was conscious. Hernando's gasp of relief was still full of shuddering sobs, like a child's.

He loves me, sighed Sam. He didn't try to pronounce it.

Enjoy took her time climbing the five flights. She always

paused at the landings to check her reflection in the security mirrors.

Hernando applied a towel full of ice to Sam's jaw and put on a jacket—Sam's jacket—over the holster.

Donegal tweed, mumbled Sam around the ice pack. So should I assume she's with me, then?

Hernando opened the apartment door. Never assume, he hissed.

Enjoy Ocasio, Hispanically beautiful, had the look of a spoiled ingenue; a road company understudy for Maria in *West Side Story*. You imagined her perpetually rehearsing "I Feel Pretty."

She proffered a freezer bag. Mango no, she explained. Her eyes flickered briefly, recording afterimages of the last scene: Sam's ice pack, slightly bloody; Hernando in a bulging jacket. Hernando never wore a jacket.

What is on? she asked, pointing her delicate chin toward the VCR, pointedly not meaning that. *Zulu* had by now been replaced by *The Return of Martin Guerre*, with the sound off. You could hear Sinéad O'Connor complaining faintly from the bedroom stereo: *Am I not your girl?* . . .

Hate that person, said Enjoy.

Sam studied her. Was she innocent? Whaddya know, Enjoy? he ventured lightly. *¿Qué sabes?*

She glanced sideways at Hernando, then sauntered purposefully into the kitchen, bearing the freezer bag as though it were a protective charm.

They both watched her glide past, Sam noting her olivine blush, her downcast eyes; Hernando focusing on her erect nipples, a subliminal message under the message T-shirt that proclaimed AUTHENTIC above the breast, ORIGINAL below.

Mocha chip or double-fudge chunk ripple? she called.

Yeah, they chorused.

There followed elaborate clinking, running water, soft Spanish curses, assorted sounds of washing up.

She reappeared with bowls, spoons, and the ice-cream containers precariously balanced on a rubber trash-bin lid. She curtsied. Good evening, señores. I am your serving wench, Nacho Dorito. These are my . . . flavors. She arched backward only slightly.

Ludo called, said Sam. Just after you did. Did you know he was going to call? What did the president know and when did he know it?

Hernando shifted on the orange sofa, but made no other move. Enjoy turned her ice-cream spoon upside-down in her mouth and licked the back. *No comprendo inglés*, she said carefully.

That means Shut up, Sam, said Hernando with a nasty smile.

Ah, said Sam. But then maybe she *is* with me. What did you do when I said Help?

When was that?

On the phone, just before Hernando busted my face with that jammy he's wearing.

Hernando unfolded with all deliberate speed and drew out the gun from its resting place. He held it flat in his open palm, gazing at it with something like wonder.

Right, he said.

What I did, said Enjoy, was I called 911. She licked the

spoon again. And gave the cops this address. Didn't I? She frowned thoughtfully, as if trying to remember. She rolled a joint, licked that too, passed it to Hernando.

Remember that time? Sam was saying softly. My mother was away and Ludo went up and slept in her bed? I tried to stop him. You were there. You were in the bed. You still are, aren't you? Both?

Baby makes three, murmured Hernando. He held the joint solemnly to the lips of one, then the other, like a communion wafer.

Zan Playfair uttered a string of schoolboy curses, rather more explicitly related to bladder and rectal functions than to rude sex. He had rubbed the windshield with the cut edge of a raw potato—the Irish cure for a broken wiper arm. The starchy juice was supposed to coat the glass so that rain would sheet off it. No hope. None for the clutch, either; he had been forced to perform Le Mans button starts at the last two test sites, and his scores had suffered.

Live the life into which you've been designed, his chum Nicky used to say. Nicky claimed to be perfectly happy, though married to an avowed nonsexual. They had quite nice silver, a distinguished old hyphenated surname, all the best invitations, and there had been no question of anything beastly in anyone's bedroom ever. Whereas here Zan was stuck in sodden Ireland with sodding Giles and a banjaxed wiper. Upon occasion, one almost wished one could envy Nicky.

How is it going, dear boy? Giles fastens the tonneau cover

deftly. Snap! Zan flashes him a dear-boyish grin, though the pony toss of hair doesn't quite make it with the rain blowing sideways.

Ludo emerges from a phone booth, somehow enlarged, like Clark Kent in his power suit. He flourishes a sleek black appointment book, the largest I've ever seen, and probably made of baby skins from the most endangered species. A silver fountain pen slides into its appointed slot, with a contented sigh.

Did you talk to someone nice? I ask lightly.

My mother, he says, unnecessary emphasis on the *mother*. All right, I'm hypersensitive. Also, I think he talked to someone else.

It's a good time to try Sam, I toss out, still light, but wavering. After midnight there.

Fine, he snaps. Send him a kiss for me. Mwa.

Sam's machine picks up. The U.S.A. direct operator cuts it off, reports curtly: It's a recording. Try later.

Please, I say, just listen to the whole message, would you? So I'll know when to call back?

She obliges. I hear it play out. He's there, I'm certain. Inches from the machine. With whom? Doing what? I begin to cry.

The last time Sam called me, he was in the usual trouble. Money, was it? Money and/or some love-light that failed.

Help, he didn't say. Just called to say hi, he insisted. Until I pleaded for the details I knew were coming. Whatever it was that time, I offered what I could. Promises, reassurances. The familiar lullaby, whose words were that he was fine and strong and beautiful, that I loved him.

He silenced me, also as usual. It's no help. It's clichés.

Clichés are truths, I protested. Clichés begin like any other epiphany. They only get dull from too much careless handling. Like people.

What do you know! he shouted. I'm desperate.

What? What? I shouted back. Can't you ever be straight with me? I need—

Oh, so it's back to you, is it? Always back to *you*!

I closed my eyes. It went on for an hour or two. He just called to say hi.

But perhaps he was calling even then from a room filled with assassins. And perhaps I was about to set out in a fast car, with one of them. Did he know? Did they plan it all?

Just say Hi, then, I whispered at the end, and hung up. Somehow when a child howls in the night, you know hunger from loneliness, colic from cold, or a violent pricking of tender flesh. Exactly when does language intercept the message, scramble the code? There was this silent movie about twin brothers separated at birth. They grew up far apart, never knowing the other existed. One gets wounded in some duel; the other bleeds from the same spot, half a world away. They cry out in unison: the wounded one and his whole, severed Other. Sam and I.

Now, here, Ludo has put on his tender smile. All right? he says, touching my shoulder.

Only then do I know how useless tears are.

I'm driving, when we come to one of those sudden Irish bridges, right-angled, stone-walled, tumbled together like an afterthought, a shrug of shoulder. The fact that death has occurred here is marked by a diamond-shaped sign, white, with a simple black spot.

I'm aware of an odd, troubling noise, like an exasperated sigh, under my left foot. I glance down, slowing to a crawl at this blind entry to the bridge. There's a single clouded flash of light in the mist, before we're hit head-on. The other car, a van brimming with mattresses, enough for a touring production of *The Princess and the Pea*. The driver is shrieking curses; his car is dead, I've killed it, I was looking at the river, he saw me, he'll forget the whole thing if I'll buy him a new car—

Ludo is a thundercloud. He's out of the car, under it, circling it. Only one headlight is smashed and a corner creased. The other car is a collapsed accordion. The stream of curses goes on, something about insurance, something about drunk drivers, drugs, tourists, bloody Brits. There's a fat woman in the van, cursing too, then whispering to the driver like a stage prompter. He changes his tone; he's willing to drive off the bridge if the van can move. They know where the *garda* station is; we'll follow them and file a report.

Ludo drives, not looking at me, not speaking. We plunge

into the darkening road, following the crippled van. Wherever it goes, it goes nowhere. After endless turns, past nothing and no one, it stops at a square outside some town. A square that resembles a set for a stalker movie: empty, desolate, squat gray tenements with no lights; streets without cars or people; a telephone box at the far end.

The fat woman struggles out of the van and lumbers toward us. The driver disappears inside the nearest blank building. Ludo mutters, I'm going to call the *gardai*, leaps from the car, and walks calmly to the telephone box. As if on cue, six or eight urchins pop out of the surrounding buildings, run after him, and press against the glass walls of the box.

As I move to the driver's seat, the woman climbs into the passenger's side.

I'm going—, I start to say.

You're not, she retorts, seizing the hand brake. Not going anywhere. Her soft fist closes around the brake as though it is a weapon.

At the end of the square I see Ludo imprisoned in his lighted glass box, like an upright Sleeping Beauty. The mob of horrible children shriek and pound their fists on the transparent walls.

There is no one else anywhere in the world. Until an old man in an anorak appears magically at the car window. He intones, with quiet menace, I am the driver. The woman beside me nods approval.

But of course he is not the driver. The man in the van was young, a wild black-haired boy with a livid scar on his cheek. He has vanished, it is clear, forever.

You are not the driver, I announce bravely to the old man. My friend is calling the police.

The woman laughs. One of the urchins, a girl of perhaps fourteen, with pale hair arranged like a crown of daggers, is racing toward us, yelling triumphantly, waving the telephone receiver, its torn metal cord whipping over her head. She throws it into our car like a grenade. I hear Ludo shouting. The shattering of glass. Now he's running toward me, waving a hand that appears to be bloody. The children disperse as swiftly as they came. The dagger-haired girl is gone, and with her the fat woman. They speed off in the crippled van, tires screaming as they take the corner.

We're not staying for the *gardai*. Ludo, in gear, blasts us off in no known direction. His hand is cut where the metal phone cord sliced across it; there are some scratches on his face as well, from the splintering of his glass cage.

We're not going to talk about it, and when I reach toward him with a handkerchief, he hits my hand away, hard enough to bring tears. Or perhaps they were already in place.

Read the map, damn you. We're in bloody Ballina. We've lost an hour.

My hands shake as I try to read, filthy road signs, pea-soup fog, insane instructions: Slide the Romer's vertical scale north or south (up or down) so that it corresponds likewise to the horizontal grid. . . .

The one-eyed car lights only the hedgerows, thickly populated with abandoned wrecks, suicidal dogs, and bicycle riders dressed in perpetual mourning for their own imminent deaths on this road.

Look! Ludo yells, exultant. It's a car, luminous as a Technicolor fantasy. Red. Glowing white top. It's the Lotus. They wave; Ludo gives them an Irish salute, like the touching of an invisible peaked cap.

We must be near the checkpoint, then, I murmur.

Not bloody likely.

But—?

I don't know why they're here, too. Maybe they followed us.

Where do you think the woman went, in the van?

Back to the bridge, I expect. After summoning an ambulance. She'll claim whiplash and sue me. She'll collect too.

And the driver?

Probably ran for his life. Tinkers. Driving without insurance. The only crime Irish men lock each other up for.

And us? Won't the police be looking for us?

He doesn't answer. But suddenly he's smiling. Cars, a lot of them. We're on the right road, we're not alone. He begins to lick his flesh wounds. I watch the rhythmic darting tongue, feeling the familiar inward lurch. I have no shame.

How come Zan followed us? I say, to shake myself free.

He's following orders.

Whose? Who is he?

Ludo's smile slides into mischief. Zan's a queen. Which outranks a princess. Except in the court of public opinion.

Another no win. Try, try again. Ludo, I say brightly. Could someone plant an explosive in a music tape? Like, time it to go off during the victim's favorite song?

What's yours? he says. I don't answer. Anyway, of course, that would be a snap. One can, don't forget, digitally create an entirely new Bogart movie just by splicing the words from all the lines he ever spoke.

Mm. Almost as neat as killing someone with a friendly call on his cellular phone. All *they* needed was a pal to pick it up and tell the victim, It's for you. His last word was Hello?

This gets a laugh. Chilling. We pull into the lunch halt, and Zan is suddenly draped over the driver's door.

What? Ludo snaps.

Hate to trouble you, old man, but we could use a hand.

Ludo yanks on the brake and climbs out.

I say, Shall I bother to wait up?

No reply to that; he's gone nearly an hour, during which I make another frantic search of the car. This time I don't hesitate to rip a seam or two, poke a finger inside door panels, seats. I even gaze helplessly at the pile of music tapes. Would I recognize anything funny? Only if it blew up.

The glove compartment yields a yellowing news feature about some of Princess Victoria's excellent adventures: hot-air ballooning, Himalayan trekking. Keeping silence in a Tibetan cloister. The pictures don't look like Zan. Much.

Tonight's halt is in a Manor House hotel. I booked it, I admit. Because it's a castle, like all Irish castles built by Brits a century or two ago. Usually by a second son who couldn't inherit the ancestral home. So he set out to make a fancy copy, with cheap labor, across the pond. It was a pretty good deal. You could buy fishing and shooting rights along with your acres. You could command any number of colleens to beat your carpets and polish your heirlooms, and strapping lads to chop your firewood and gillie your sporting guests. You'd never trust one of them with a key to the wine cellar, but you could teach them to roast a decent joint and bake a treacle tart every bit as cloying as the ones you'd had in school.

The years have been good to Irish castles. After independence, the Brits began unloading them—those that weren't torched. Hotel chains bought them, the church turned a few into convents, and some descendants hung on for dear life, trying to keep them heated, running them as bed-and-breakfasts. Impoverished earls can now be found making change at their castles' front doors. The tourists love it—they are the American descendants of the locals who used to be the cook, the maid, and the kid who climbed the garden wall to steal apples.

It's still fun to stay in these places, if you don't give it all too much thought. It's fun to watch the staff make up the rooms: two girls working as a team, for speed and efficiency—and to control snooping, not to mention theft. The Manor House inns still tuck you in snugly, in two or three woollen blankets wrapped around the sagging mattress. The eiderdowns get a good shake. The girls whisper and giggle over curly hairs in the tub, sex stains in the bed linens, exotic "smalls" hanging on the heated towel bars.

This hostelry had added a new wing, sleek and modern, with nasty carpets that smelled of petrochemicals, and furniture that gleamed without polish.

We asked for the old wing. There was only one suite available. I didn't look at Ludo; he must have nodded. A

red-faced boy in a shiny-buttoned uniform led us, miles, it
seemed, up and down stairs and at last to a big room filled
with linen cabbage roses, mahogany, tufted velvet, canopied
four-poster, and a magnificent old harpsichord whose keys
were the color of George Washington's fine wooden teeth.

Bath? Ludo inquired, frisky as a puppy. Yes, please. Off he
trotted to run one. Champagne? Before or after? During, I
said. It was duly summoned and delivered. He poured and
set the chilled flutes on the rim of the foaming tub.

Lovely, I said.

In, he commanded. I obeyed. He followed. I closed my
eyes. He kissed them.

Can I ask you something? I managed to say.

Hmm. Not just at the moment.

The bath cooled, bubbles of foam subsided with gentle
whispers. Champagne slid icily from one mouth to another,
warming as it flowed.

Nice? he whispered. Happy? No answer.

Fingertips on my breast, expert, insistent, coaxing the response without words. There. Having made his point, he
rose with the foam. My eyes were still closed, but I felt his
gaze moving over me like another touch. Warm and cool at
once. A driving force.

You had a question, he said.

No. No.

Time passed. And he, and I. The bath grew cold. I open
my eyes. His mouth and his cock are turning lavender blue,
the color of sterling silver roses. We are still swimming in the
dying bubbles, and then he is suddenly gone—splashing,

toweling, leaving a trail of shining footprints. Hurry! His voice has no trace of shared secrets. Starving! he calls from the bedroom. I hurry. He's already dressed, the door to the corridor just clicking shut behind him. Abandoned: champagne, cigarette stub smoldering in a crystal ashtray, me. He has erased the hour. Only my body would swear that we spent it together. And my body is a hostile witness.

Downstairs in the pub lounge a tightish knot of our fellow travelers are tucking back bourbon and red, shandy, Guinness, hot Irish with cloves and sugar. Wisps of war stories about fog and dicky brakes drift in and out of the smoke. Ludo and Zan are wedged in a corner; they don't see me, I don't see Giles. I stay where I am, studying their intent faces, easy hand gestures. They are not strangers. I can't decide what they are.

On the other hand, what do I know about male bonding? Maybe they're just attracted to each other's cars. I'm still pondering when I see Zan's elbow glide smoothly into Ludo's ribs. Ludo looks up, catches my eye, waves. Before I move, there's a foot of space between them. Lightning reaction time. Rally drivers.

Sam can hear his mom's voice, arguing with the operator. I feel so distant, he says, drawing out the so-o-o, expecting a laugh.

Enjoy makes a sound, possibly sympathetic. Hernando has his earphones on; he's giggling to his private music.

Latins are lousy lovers, Sam mutters.

Huh, says Enjoy. You wish.

Sam glares at her. So are you guys supposed to off me or what?

Her shrug is purely eloquent.

Hey, he says urgently. Aren't you going to help me?

She turns her black eyes on him, like a negative flash. What do I get? Risk my life?

You want money? he ventures.

She giggles. How about that silver clock in your mom's bedroom? The one that tells time in colors.

Shit, says Sam. Fucking *clock*? We're discussing my life here.

Enjoy shrugs again, causing an abrupt shift between the words AUTHENTIC and ORIGINAL stretched across her T-shirted breasts.

Anyway, what's Hernando getting? Who's paying him? Ludo? Shit! The three of you are my only friends.

Hernando has disconnected his earphones. So what are friends for? he says, laughing. Like, a guy's got no friends, who you gonna get to sell him out? His *mom*?

Sam begins to whimper.

Hey, Enjoy says. Hey, don't. She looks up guiltily at Hernando. Okay to make a sympathetic noise? Not okay? he doesn't seem to notice. He is rubbing the bloodstains on his silk sleeve. Rhythmically, back and forth, to no avail.

The phone rings again. This time no one glances at it. After eight rings, the machine picks up. The caller leaves no message.

Sam asks: Will you at least tell me when?

Hernando's earphones are back in place. His head jerks lazily; he pops a new laser disc in the machine: *Road Warrior*. Sam tries not to watch. Enjoy? he says softly. What's he getting? Who's paying? When?

She begins to move away. Dishes to do, cats to feed, laundry in the machine.

My mom, Sam persists, could pay more. Maybe a lot more. If she knew. If you could let her—

Hernando is unplugged. He looms over Sam, swaying like a nervous boxer, shifting his weight. Then he wheels, swinging, cursing in Spanish, punching the air. Enjoy stumbles backward, scattering plates, sinking to her knees with her hands over her head. Hernando drops to her side, examining the shards of white china with pale blue flowers. He selects one, seizes Enjoy's hand, draws the jagged point across, as though he were slicing fruit. All three of them stare at the thin red line against the pale skin of her palm.

Hernando refastens his earphones and focuses his attention on the film. In which life is a murderous car chase. Everyone drives. Everyone kills or is killed.

Enjoy's hand is streaming; she utters no sound, but begins to sweep up the mess, making it worse as she goes. Edging past Sam with the ghastly dustpan, she manages to mouth two words: I'll try.

THREE

~✓~

H.R.H. Victoria Anne is here, in this room. I keep telling myself it is none of my business. That I could die trying to save her. That Sam could die too, possibly not even knowing why. That Ludo is not even a monster. He is only a beautiful machine, like his car. Anyone can drive it.

He sits opposite me in this elegant dining room, with his stockinged foot in my lap, warm toes exploring me under the white tablecloth, as if they were delivering some urgent, passionate message. Meanwhile his restless hands are on the table. He is drawing pictures in the corners of the menu. Classic cars in motion, classic airplanes in flight. The drawings are precise, meticulous renderings of sleek engines designed for the love of dangerous sport. Or of war, which is, he explains, merely the original, most beautiful, dangerous sport. He is particularly fond of German war planes. He knows exactly where the struts go, and the angle of the wings, just as he knows every detail of the instrument panel of the first Alfa. His draftsmanship is extraordinary. He sketches, drinks, smokes, smiles, talks, drums bored fingers on the cloth. All the while, toes insinuate themselves deftly into the silken creases of my silk trousers, urging my body to hum along with all his rhythms, the crazy rhythms, I suddenly think, of a hyperactive head-banging child.

Are you happy? he blurts suddenly, looking utterly sweet, a little boy unsure if his bouquet of wildflowers will please. Perhaps I am allergic.

If my life depends on my answer, and it may, I would have to confess. Happy. I am. Ludo of the lapwings.

Frowning, he resumes his drawing. A fuselage? A Fokker? He turns the drawing around. Look, he says. It's you, driving. See—dark hair flowing, long scarf trailing in the wind.

I turn the menu and push it back. Trailing scarf, I say, is how Isadora Duncan died.

Sometimes I need help too, he says. The voice has gone very quiet.

But H.R.H. Victoria Anne is in this room. I say it to myself again and again, like a mantra. Once there was an exotic cigarette slogan: Someone in this room is smoking Gauloises. And I intend to meet him.

My eyes wander, to distract me from the warmth in my groin, from the beautiful face so absorbed in his restless doodling. I fasten my gaze on every face but his. Scrutineering. Avenger Tiger; the elderly couple whose car is a Mini Moke;

the fat aliens driving a fifties Nash Rambler. Well, it is a classic car of sorts. Its foldout backseat bore almost as much blame for America's sexual revolution as Brando's undershirt, Elvis's hips. This Rambler's crew is from Devonshire. Two lager louts with flaming cheeks. All that air and clotted cream.

No chance they're fakes.

Well, but the girls from Belfast. Or Zan and Giles. I'm getting drowsy.

Darling? Ludo's foot prods. He says again, Darling?

Help.

Want to—go upstairs?

Mm, I murmur. Not too committal.

You go on, then, he says. I'll be along.

Click.

Calls to make? I ask. How about we make one together?

He frowns, but checks his watch. Then he smiles, as if he's bestowing a gift. Why not? It is a gift.

We inhabit the elegant mahogany booth in the lobby, a snug sarcophagus for two.

He passes the time tracing my nipples through my shirt, testing for signals. I pull away. He laughs.

Sam's machine picks up. We wait for the "no one can take your call . . ." But instead there is a musical giggle, followed by a female voice. *Hola, mama.* Happy birthday. Life begins at forty, *¿verdad?* Then the beep.

Ludo is clearly perplexed. I'm trying to crack the code. Life begins at forty. It *is* Sam's birthday, but he's twenty-nine. Forty? Thousand dollars? For Sam's life?

I say, What was that—a wrong number? Let me try—

He hesitates. Then redials. U.S.A. direct. This time it's the usual message. He seems relieved, but not entirely. Possibly he knew that other voice. He says into the phone: We cool or what? But of course there is no reply. He studies me thoughtfully; I am blank, scared, bewildered. Those are all good. Meanwhile my brain races my heartbeat. Could I get enough money? Where? And where to? What if it's some trick—Sam and Ludo, some drug deal? It could happen. And I can't afford to think that.

Ludo nudges me out of the booth, back to the hotel pub. I get to search the crowd once more. The TV crew edges toward Ludo, waving their mops and boxes. There he is, the comic relief of this event. So where have you been all day? they want to know.

Lost, says Ludo, wearing his sweet, sheepish grin, the one that slides from aw-shucks to naughty-boy in the twinkling of the twinkling. Their cameras eat him up. And he disappears.

Avenger Tiger is at my elbow, waving his dog-eared rally map. How you keeping? he says.

But for you it would be two days ago. In another country. I mean it.

Drink? he offers. I check him out for ulterior motives, possible disguises. Not too princessy. Although—

Hot Irish, I say. With cloves. And I won't even ask you to mark my escape route.

I will if you like.

I may if you would. Do I keep calling you Tiger?

Mutch, he says, holding out his left hand. The right is jammed deep in his coat pocket.

Mutch something? Or something Mutch? Mutch ado would be fun.

Not Mutch for me. His smile is nice. I raise my glass to it. Gap between the front teeth always gets me.

I know it's your first rally, he's saying. Is it your last, d'you think?

I'm afraid so. The gravity of my tone surprises us both. So I laugh. He looks at me curiously. They do say it's a crucible, he is saying. Take any two people—lock in a tight, airless container. Send them hurtling—he shakes his head—I mean, even if they're best friends. Lovers?

Tell me about it. I roll my eyes. This is instead of answering that last question. He doesn't press. I finish my hot whiskey and start looking for Ludo.

One more?

Too sweet. Besides, I should— But Ludo is not to be found.

Mutch is checking my expression. So? he says. Time for another one after all. Right?

No—yes. I'm startled at how grateful I feel. Thanks very—Mutch. He winces. Sorry.

And you are? Just in case we can crack wise about that.

I consider inventing a persona. Wouldn't be the first time. Vicky, I say.

Try again. His face has gone all dark, as though I'd thrown an off switch. Anyway, you're Mary Jo. At least it says so on the entry list. Wasn't that the girl Ted Kennedy drowned in a car?

My turn to wince. No relation.

Well, at least we're even, he says. All of a sudden his smile is not so nice. Besides, he's flashing it over my left shoulder. I hate that.

Say hello to my co-driver, he says. John Joe, Mary Jo. No relation.

We all pretend to be glad to meet. John Joe has tousled black hair and ice blue eyes. Classic Northern Irishman. Like Black Jack Bouvier, Jackie Kennedy's no-good dad. Also, I suddenly remember, like the van driver who crashed into us and then took off. I'm looking for the scar. Probably combs his hair that way to cover it.

You must be the Avenger, I say.

He looks blank. Mutch? he says. I'm gone.

Mutch barely nods. Righti-o.

Somehow you never think of the navigator as the brains of the outfit. I feel better suddenly. If I had a saddle, I'd stand taller in it.

John Joe vanishes. Again?

That was Vicky, says Mutch. Thought you'd want to know.

Bollocks. But I'm shaken, and he can tell. Plus his right hand is still jammed in that pocket.

Today's papers, Irish, British, and U.S., are thoughtfully stacked at the reception desk. I scoop up a random selection and stand there scanning front pages, news index, sports section. Everyone has a brief update on the rally. Opening-day bomb scare, coincidence of the blown-up bridge at Newry, dwindling number of competing cars, rotten weather, history of the event . . .

With forty-eight hours to go, officials express confidence

that our troubles are behind us. Local *gardai* remain on alert at test sites, checkpoints, control stations, night halts. In addition, unmarked security vehicles have been dispatched to undisclosed points along the route. I smile. Won't help those of us who keep getting lost, will it?

The big story is peace talks. Men in suits gathering to talk about money and stability, about Ireland safe and sound. Burger King is coming, and Tower Records. Didn't they conquer Moscow? Won't they fit right in on the Shankhill road? Wait—where are these guys meeting? Not in Belfast, but the Midlands. And who else is going to the Midlands? Oh, God. Oh, Christ.

If I call Sam now, what message can I leave on the infernal machine? Funny, that was what they used to call a time bomb. I rehearse a few Hallmark greetings. I could whistle something. A war song? "Over There"? He wouldn't get it. "Danny Boy"? "Sonny Boy"? I'm still standing near the booth, minding my own desperate business, and I feel someone behind me, watching. Not too close. I know not to turn around.

The glass wall of the booth reflects me, damask sofas, the concierge with his gold epaulets, standing tall behind his white marble. And beyond him, a dark blur of someone moving. I can just catch the color, distorted by the darkness behind the glass. It seems red, scarlet, burgundy. I turn slightly, enough to spot a fast-moving woman, one of the Belfast girls in the battered Reliant. Little Red Riding Hood. She tosses a glance over her shoulder; our eyes meet; she keeps moving, so I make haste, catch up, pluck at her sleeve. Hey, I say, exhaling harmless goodwill. So how's it going?

She is not similarly inclined. In fact, she glowers as though she were a holdup person and I a security camera. I'm Mary Jo, I persist, Mary Jovially. We met at the gas station near Ranelagh? Esso, I believe. You were rattling on. My co-driver is Ludo?

Lu-do? she echoes, registering an exaggerated blank. Oh, yeah. You're—

The hostage? I offer. Pawn, patsy, dupe? Fall guy.

I don't understand. Her eyes are darting.

Look, I say. Someone I love could be dying.

Same here, she snaps with sudden, vehement coldness. We can't help each other. Sorry.

As she turns, I whisper, Vicky? She keeps walking.

I duck into the phone booth and dial U.S.A. direct.

Sorry, I can't take your . . .

I wait for the beep. Yo, I say. I just called to say hi.

Ludo is pressed against the glass, not looking too much like a kid with a yen for candy. He pushes the door in. Anyone nice?

I try a dazzling smile. Just some royal pain—

He grabs my arm. More trouble, he says.

Than I'm worth, you mean?

Look, I've had it. Go up and pack your gear, we're leaving. He says something else, under his breath.

Please, I say. For the life of me I can't finish the sentence.

So I do what I'm told. He follows me within minutes, picks up his suitcase. It's already packed. Your turn with the bill, he says on the way out.

That's a break. I could ask the concierge to ring U.S.A. direct after I'm gone. The message, madam? Just say Hi.

Or I could leave a note at the desk for Mutch: Follow that car. But he never did say whether it was Mutch something or something Mutch.

I get to the parking lot first. The silver car glows like a moon. Ludo appears at the top of the magnificent stone staircase, framed by ancient carriage lanterns. I can't help it, I'm photographing him walking down those steps in milky dawn light. Lugging champagne in a gold plastic carry bag, wearing his preposterous black suede cowboy jacket, with the fringes. And his all-purpose don't-talk-to-me look. Which of course covers: I don't care how gorgeous I am, don't ask me to stop while you snap the shutter, and stop looking at me that way, can't you. What happened between us three hours ago never happened, or maybe I just erased the tape, which means it as good as never happened.

All the same, I keep staring and snapping, trying to focus through tears, as if the click of the shutter can restore the truth and the beauty of this Lucifer descending.

He reaches the bottom step and pauses, favoring me with a curt: Get in.

We're not due at passage control until—I wave my road book.

No penalty for early arrival, he says. I've got a stop to make.

We're doing 90 before I dare ask where.

Oh, sorry. We're going to pick up my messages.

Will they— I change my mind. Will they be serving refreshments? Are they expecting me?

No. Yes.

Really? Who are they?

Some guys. I don't know how many. Look for a sign, Knockalla Coast road. It'll be on your side.

Will they be wearing suede fringes like those? Or balaclavas over their faces?

I doubt fringes. Balaclavas I think only for active duty.

He's kidding? Not kidding? I break down.

Shit, he says. I *asked* you to look at the road.

I am, it's there, look.

We take the turn. He calms down. I stop crying. Could you just tell me what Sam's connection is? And mine? Can't I even know what I'm doing here?

He hesitates a beat, slows down, looking for whatever he needs to look for. You don't need to know. You only need to be here, of your own free will, with me. And you are, are you not.

It's a declarative statement.

False pretenses, I mutter.

Oh, really. He swerves sharply. Here it is. Signpost: Unapproved Road. The single high beam slides over it, and I steal a glance at him; again, predictably, no visible reaction. Although his emotions, as the critic once said about the famous actress, always run the gamut from A to B. In Ludo's case, no reaction is extreme action. The gamut from A to B is infinite and inhuman. A forlorn child seeking asylum inside a death mask.

This road is long, narrow, and full of sudden bends. Solid hedgerows either side reach to the tops of our windows; we're literally tunneling. The sodden hump between the ruts where our wheels go is high enough for the thick mat of weeds to choke the hand-brake cable, if not the entire underbelly of the chassis. We seem to crawl, yet mud spatters us as if we were traveling at breakneck speed. I can scarcely breathe.

We're here, he announces. A rotted-out stone bulk of a cottage, dark, windowless, the roof more holes than thatch. Two figures crouch in the doorway.

Found it, then, one calls, aiming a flashlight into our eyes.

Ludo jumps out, disappears inside with one of the welcoming party. The other stays rooted to his spot, keeping the blinding light on me, still strapped inside the car.

Excuse me? I call. I need a bathroom? A . . . loo?

Sorry, he says. No facilities.

Okay. Actually, I only wanted to hear the voice. Male. Proper Brit or Anglo accent. So what do I make of that?

Almost at once, Ludo emerges, hurrying toward me, something bulky inside his jacket. He tosses a second something to me. It's an envelope. Not to worry, he says. Won't explode. Think I'd blow up my car in a place like this?

Who knows? I say. Maybe there's enough in your other parcel to replace it.

This? He pats his pocket. Just some excellent stuff to go with the champers. In case we win the rally. You remember the rally.

He starts the engine, backs halfway down the corkscrew hill before he can turn. He's really great in reverse.

Open yours now, he says when we reach the warning signpost and turn back onto the proper paved road.

My fingers are shaking. I make a mess of the envelope; even the contents are ripped. It's a handwritten fax in Sam's writing. No mistaking that incurable left-hander's hook. It's still a kid's writing. Every word a testament to that hopeless struggle, that surrender.

When you get this, there's only one day left. Unless you help. Don't blame L. It's my fault. I love you.

What help? I say to Ludo. Steady voice; I'm proud of that.

Your money and your life.

Wasn't it your money *or* your life?

I guess it's been updated.

I wait for him to elaborate. But the sky lightens and we speed in silence along the tarmac, onto the wide public road with its normal, life-affirming signs: Children Crossing, Blind Entry, No Overtaking, Road Liable to Subside.

We pull up to the control stop from the wrong direction— a twenty-point penalty. Legitimate early birds are already lined up ahead. We are also the only car covered in mud. Ludo hops out with a cloth and does what he can. A few curious eyes take it in: Zan and Giles, spotless as always, look amused. Mutch, who didn't get my SOS because I didn't know how to address it. The TV crew, who pass us by—a first. And the time-control official, who stamps our arrival without comment.

You're not going to explain, then, I said finally.

All in good time, darling. He stroked my damp hair. Feel like driving? Here, take it.

We switched, I gunned. He frowned but said nothing, studiously reading the map. T-junction three-tenths of a mile Signpost Bally. Right here, BURMAH petrol station, watch it. I've warned you about swerving for bloody dogs. You'll kill us.

I will?

Well, *I* won't. Think I'd leave all that Veuve-Clicquot for the sweepers? Besides, imagine me going to hell without a car wash?

Imagine going in suede fringes, I mutter. For which I get a look, and resolve not to speak again.

Concentrate on driving. The morning roads still treacherous, slick with last night's rain. Even on a dry day, puddles last till noon. You pull away from a cow or a tourist on a bike, your brakes fail, you skid into a rude conversation with a telegraph pole. Call the *gardai* for help, and they send you a bill for the pole. I know.

Suddenly Ludo says Sam and I owe some money. To some guys.

Some.

Fair amount. This was a way to pay it all.

What was? My gaze is fixed on the YIELD sign, the farmhouse, two schoolgirls in their navy pinafores. Road forks, one half mile, take a left.

This job, he says.

Murder.

Hopefully not. Scaring some people. Big time.

So what am I, a decoy? I plant the—thing?

Not exactly.

Are we carrying it?

Not exactly.

Is—she really in this race? Do you know? Why are they holding Sam?

She is, I do, because you have to do your bit. And it's the only way to make sure. I promise he'll be safe. Trust me? You ought to.

As he talks, I can see him pulling a slender coiled wire from inside his jacket. Looks like a Slinky toy.

That's the—is it? The wheel jerks.

Eyes on the road, he says. It's a solenoid. For the brakes. They're soft. Test them yourself.

I press the pedal; all the way down. No response. I have to stop! I yell. You drive. You've done something to it. I'm going to be sick.

You're not, he says. You drive till I tell you to stop. Use the hand brake.

I try it. Nothing. That road—this morning—it must have snapped.

Ease up. Coast. We're coming to a hill.

I spin the wheel and steer into the ditch. Shaking and sobbing, I climb out and throw up.

Shit, he says, but not angrily. Here, hold this. It's his jacket. He dives under the car, into the mud, with the toolbox. I wish I thought he really was fixing the hand brake cable. I wish I could tell a solenoid from a detonator. I try to keep thinking, No way he'd destroy this car. It helps a little.

There's a house fifty yards ahead. I've got to pee, I say. Behind those bushes. I point.

Don't do anything I wouldn't have Sam shot for. This is

said amiably, so I laugh. I go behind the bushes. When I get back he's in the car, testing the brakes. They respond.

What did you do?

Oh, wiggle, wiggle, he says. Almost always does the trick.

Solenoid, I say. Solenoid? Someone who's paranoid about the sun?

About *her* son, he says. I hate the smile that comes with it.

A red Lotus pulls up behind us. Zan waves without slowing down. Need help? Spirit of the Event. No thanks, Ludo calls, but the sound disappears in the roar of their exhaust. Seconds later, the Reliant pulls up and stops. Problems? says Gwyneth. (I've looked her up.) I say, No brakes.

Never use 'em, she says gaily. Wears 'em out.

We know, says Ludo. Thanks.

Have you heard? yells Niamh, the slightly butch co-driver. It's pronounced Knave. Some princess is driving the Clan Crusader. We passed it back there, six minutes ago.

Very precise, these rally folks.

Quick check of my entry list. It's got Royal R. R. Riley driving the Crusader. B. Jones co-driver.

Royal? I say aloud. Not too imaginative, eh? But cute.

Ludo's head shake is firm, authoritative. Couldn't happen. Not a Crusader. No way.

I can't resist. We could hang for six minutes and check it out.

He hesitates. Nah. But then he releases the hood catch and climbs out again. More tinkering. And he'd said it was all fixed. Wiggle, wiggle. He's still there five and a half minutes later when the black Crusader moves into view. Then he's up like a shot, brandishing tools. The black car slows to a stop. Spirit of the Event.

Trouble? shouts the putative Royal R. R. Riley.

Ludo grins. Wouldn't have a torque wrench, would you?

Riley hops out, rummages in his trunk. He and Ludo huddle under the lid. Things go clunk. I keep a respectful distance. B. Jones, Riley's co-driver, shakes hands, offers a smoke, doesn't speak. He sports a trim beard and a slight paunch. Late forties. Could be a fake beard. Could just B. Jones. I turn back to study Riley's deliciously presented rear end. Buns of steel. Leather boots gleam expensively. Too nice for this terrain. I hear him swear softly, can't place the accent. When at last he straightens up and bangs the lid shut, I gasp. He's wearing suede, with fringes. It's brown, but still. On the other hand, maybe this is just a hot look for rally drivers. What do I know? I squint, but he's too quick; he and Ludo nod, salute, separate. He's in his car and gone.

So much for wiggle, wiggle, I mutter. Ludo reclaims the driver's seat.

I gather the Crusader was worth the wait, I say.

Read the map, will you.

One-half mile road forks. Signpost Gortafludig left. So what did you guys talk about? Or did you just put your Slinky in her boot?

He chortles. You do make things sound sexy, don't you.

I'm sure it is sexy. Death in the Afternoon. Death and the Maiden. Though of course she's hardly.

Who's hardly what?

77

Vicky. A maiden. Three-tenths of a mile. Graveyard. Hang a right.

He digs out a tape from the pile at my feet. Vivaldi enfolds us, heralds our coming, trails in our wake, piercing the steel gray mist with shafts of light. Sheep grazing the long acre look up in brief astonishment.

Ludo, shielded by his music, smokes and increases speed, steering the wheel with his knees.

Look, Ma, no hands. I don't look.

F O U R

~⌣~

Hernando is cooking spaghetti when the call comes. Enjoy's blood seeps through the bandage they made by ripping up Sam's Tower Records T-shirt. They've given her enough marijuana to stop her crying, but she can hardly stand.

This is the day, Sam says, checking his wrist before he remembers; Hernando is now wearing the gold watch, Sam's grandfather's. I removed it in the funeral home. Before this is over, Hernando will own everything of Sam's he has ever coveted. Except possibly Enjoy. Though she was never really anyone's to covet.

I'm hungry, she whimpers. Can't we get a pizza or something? I hate spaghetti.

You got any cash? Hernando snaps.

She shakes her head weakly.

Sam says, Use my credit card.

Right. I'll call. Mushroom okay? says Enjoy.

Sausage, says Hernando.

You don't eat carcass anymore, Sam reminds him.

I forgot, says Hernando. Okay, mushroom.

Hernando's spaghetti water is boiling over. He curses, deals with it. Then, earphones in place, he begins to stir the sauce, head bobbing in sync with the red bubbles.

Enjoy makes the call.

When the buzzer rings, they all jump as though they hadn't been waiting for it.

Hernando answers. Yeah?

Pizza for Sam, uh, looks like Munchkin? Or maybe that's the order.

Close enough. Be right down. Hernando has thoughtfully ripped up another shirt to tie them hand to foot while he goes to collect the food. He does it now, careful not to get any more of Enjoy's blood on the silk shirt.

He races down the five flights, opens the three doors and the security gate, with Sam's key.

The pizza man smiles. Sam?

Yeah, says Hernando, flourishing gold plastic.

The man studies the card, shifts his pile of white boxes, produces a portable credit card machine and a ballpoint.

Forging Sam's name, Hernando suddenly slumps forward and crumples to the pavement without a sound.

The pizza man pockets his machine, ballpoint, and Sam's card, removes Sam's watch, and slips quickly into the darkness of East Sixth Street. The stack of pizza boxes gleams in his arms like some unearthly art object, until he deposits them all in a corner trash can. Only then does he begin to run.

A Federal Express box addressed to me is waiting at the front desk of the Castle Arms.

We had in fact tried to book at the Georgian House, across the road, where the prize-giving ceremony would be held. But that was also where the peace talks were happening, and it was awash in diplomatic staff and media. All we had to dodge at the Castle Arms was a convention of chefs hunting wild fungi and an art-film crew shooting forty shades of green in the Kerry Mountains.

I rip open my package; it's Sam's watch. Crystal smashed, hands stopped at 10:15, New York time. Ludo's expression is shock. But I can hardly trust Ludo's expression. Bastard. Bastard. I can't scream, can't attack him. I only stand there, frozen, gulping air, holding on to the black marble slab where it says WELCOME, staring at the clerk's smile. He proffers a key with a brass disk. If I can just get you to sign—

Ludo's grip on my shoulders is unshakable. You've got to believe me.

I feel myself slide out of his grasp anyway. I can hardly hear his voice through the screaming in my head.

It's some ghastly trick, he is shouting. It's not true, I swear.

Down on the polished stone floor the world feels cool and strangely beautiful. Distant whispers of well-shod feet moving on thick carpets the color of blood. Murmurs of polite concern, wary offers of water, air, an escort to my room. After all, I may be simply drunk, or looking to sue the hotel. It's a growth industry, even here.

They must have got me to the room somehow, because I'm in bed, and Ludo is beside me, sponging my face with a cool cloth. He looks so worried.

What do you want? I say. For God's sake.

You have to know; you have to. I'd never let Sam be hurt. There are actual tears on his face. His hands are trembling. He's rolling a cigarette. Fingers and tongue so deft on the delicate tissue. I close my eyes so I don't have to watch, don't have to let it remind me of other deft things he does with fingers and tongue.

So you didn't issue any order. Let's say that. Let's say I believe that. He is dead, though. Somehow, somebody managed to kill him. What do you want with me? Now.

Not a lot, he sighs. It never was such a lot.

Now, though? Now that I have no earthly reason to do anything at all, except maybe pay you back? Somehow.

If I can prove to you Sam is not dead. If I can prove that, will you help me, help him? Sure, I say dully. Why wouldn't I. He puts the watch in my hand, closes my fingers over it. My father's old timepiece; my son's. It's started ticking again. I reset it. Ludo turns the lights out and leaves, wearing his fringed suede. I hear him lock the door from outside. I lie still, holding this lump of gold, listening to the tick. Three A.M., New York time.

The scrape of the key in the door, the clank of that brass disk, wake me. No idea of the time. Ludo?

But it isn't Ludo. It's Mutch. He announces this as he bursts in. Someone with him. They switch on the light, blinding me. The one who isn't Mutch is wearing a balaclava.

I consider the telephone. Mutch says, Don't. No point, d'you see. You've no choice. None of us has.

I do, I say. Doesn't matter anymore.

Forgetting something, he says.

Sam's dead. Whoever did it sent me his watch. Look— But now I can't find it.

Well, he's not all that dead, Mary Jo. We heard from him less than an hour ago.

I sink back across the vast bed, diagonally, claiming it all, flinging my limbs out like a swastika. Whatever he's saying I don't want to hear.

I taped the call, Mutch persists. Here. *Listen.* He holds out a palm-size machine; flicks it on. Sam's voice gasping, faint, scared. His voice. I'm all right. Tell them. For God's sake will you at least tell— Then a click.

For an electric instant I believe it. Then I know I can't. When was it made? What if he didn't live another second past that terrifying click? I don't say a word of this. Mutch knows what I think, however. He puts a hand on my shoulder. His left, of course. The right is still in hiding. Is that a rod in your pocket? I blurt suddenly. Then I can't resist the rest of the line: Or are you just glad to see me? He doesn't crack a smile. I do; I even start to laugh, before it turns into choking sobs.

He draws out the right hand, holds it up. It's missing the

last two fingers. That crooked smile I thought I liked flashes across his face. Then he raises both hands, cocks the index fingers toward me, like a salute, or a pair of toy guns.

The tape is real, he says. And current.

Why don't we call him back? The voice that asks this surprises me. It's calm, sweet, seems to float gently from behind the velvet drapes, like theme music for a movie love scene. It's my voice. Please, it says.

The person who isn't Mutch, who has been standing at silent, rigid attention, now barks through the thick wool of his face mask. No way, he says.

Shut it, Mutch barks back—what harm? It'll help her do what—what she's got to do. He picks up the telephone and dials. U.S.A. direct. There's ringing. Someone picks up. Mutch here, he says. Can you get the kid to call us? He gives the hotel number, the room number, the time. That's all.

As he talks, my eyes remain fixed on his pale face. Trying to read it. Failing. By the time he hangs up, with a curt nod and that half-smile, I'm beyond reason. No more voice, just the choking sobs, which now hurt my throat, and which seem close to hysteria.

That won't help, Mutch snaps, but then softens his tone and starts again. They have to track him with pagers, and get him to ring back. Could take some time.

Track where—

He shrugs, turns to his partner. They exchange some swift, silent signal with their heads, their shoulders. The mystery partner starts for the door, tugging at his balaclava. I guess he can't go out in the hall wearing it. Such a simple, lightweight, all-purpose item: protection, anonymity, and menace. Stuff it in your pocket and presto! you're normal. Imagine the Crimean War, where it started. Some freezing English soldier cut up his sweater and pulled it over his head. Suddenly there was a whole army of them. Just eyes and noses. In Balaclava. Just like this.

Mutch dumps Ludo's clothes on the floor, settles uneasily in the easy chair. One leg jiggles incessantly. He is a wild boy-o with time to kill. He spots the TV remote; it will have to do. Surfing till he finds the American rock channel. A news crawl on the bottom of the busy screen. Peace talks in Ireland. Sports, weather, stock market, movie star birthdays.

The door key jangle makes him sit up straight. Ludo barely glances at either of us. Where is—everybody?

Mutch says nothing.

Ludo checks his watch. I notice he's wearing Sam's, broken crystal notwithstanding. He must have come back for it while I was asleep. Then I notice his hair is sopping. So is the suede jacket, fringes hanging like strands of a wet floor mop. He heads toward the bathroom, shedding clothes, leaving muddy tracks on the carpet.

Mutch turns back to MTV. A black girl with thick blond braids connected to her nose ring. Singing about wanting some fun. She's got a feeling she's not the only one.

Ludo shouts from the shower: Would you ever get me some dry clothes. I jump up, assuming the command is for me. Mutch's left fist whips out and smashes me in the midsection. Stunning. Breathtaking. Until now I never really understood those words.

Then he's up, pulling out drawers, flinging Ludo's silver brushes, spilling designer toiletries on the bed, the floor. He picks up a shirt, trousers, rolls them into a ball, bangs on the bathroom door, and heaves the bundle inside. Clouds of steam embrace him as he slams the door on Ludo's curses.

I fold my arms carefully across my ribs, and begin to examine myself for damage. Maybe it will only hurt when I breathe.

Bit of the rough, says Mutch, watching me. Sorry.

What did I do?

Sudden moves, he explains. I still get a bit nervy.

Ludo joins us, trying to smooth his rumpled pants, carrying Mutch's choice of shirt, fishing another out of the discard pile. I see him take in my condition, with no discernible change of expression. Leave her the fuck alone, he snarls, however. My hero.

Mutch quietly picks up a bottle of Ludo's champagne, smashes it open against the TV, pours the contents over the stuff on the bed, into the open suitcase. The Prince of Wales checkered suit. The beautiful ties, each worth about a week on the dole in Ireland.

Ludo has the presence, the sheer force of will, not to react. The telephone rings. He picks up. Sam? *Sam.* All the color drains from his face; he drops onto the sodden bed; Christ, he is actually weeping. He tosses the phone to me. I hold it to my ear as though I expect it to explode. Then I hear Sam's voice. Truly, his; alive. Where—? is all I manage to say.

Can't tell you that. But you—do what they ask. What*ever*. Promise me.

Oh, God. And I dissolve. He's alive. I will do anything.

Ludo marooned in the chaos of the sodden bed, like some dazed shipwreck. Tears course silently down his face. In spite of everything I put my arms around him. Mutch stares. God knows what he makes of it. The three of us are freeze-framed, players in a game of statues. When the door bursts open, we jump-start like a trio of adulterers caught in flagrante.

Two balaclavas storm in, the one from before, the other, also familiar, wearing fringes. It's the Crusader driver, I'm almost certain, though I barely had one glimpse of him, rear view only. Nobody speaks. The fringed one signals to Ludo; they step outside, leaving the door open a crack; I hear their voices, low at first, then coiling upward in spirals of anger. I imagine they are arguing about me; whether I'm to be killed if I don't follow orders, or maybe even if I do; whether Ludo has to do it.

He comes back in alone. Still pale, almost chalk white, but no more tears. And he doesn't look at me. Which convinces me I'm right about the quarrel. Mutch takes off without a word. Hugs or no hugs, I suppose they all trust Ludo to do the necessary.

I decide to bite the bullet. Ludo? I begin lightly. What's my assignment?

No reply. I repeat the question. Why not tell me? What harm?

You'll know when you need to.

I do better, I say, when I'm prepared. Don't you?

He tosses me a folded newspaper. I glance at the front-page photo, seven men and a woman in suits and smiles. PEACE HOPES RISE, U.S. ENVOY JOINS TALKS.

Am I supposed to kill one of these? Which one—the American? The woman?

He shakes his head. Your, uh, the details are still being discussed.

By whom? Who's in charge of me? Is it you? Will it be you if I screw up?

Stop this, he says. It'll be all right. Sam will, for sure.

I venture a sharp, contemptuous look. You're not even in charge of Sam. You thought he was dead.

I told you I didn't believe it.

And you were lying. When you heard his voice just now, on the phone, you were as shocked as I was. I *saw* you. So don't give me any promises. What I could use is one straight answer. What am I doing here?

All right. It's really very simple. Sam owes money to some . . . friends of mine. I use the word loosely. Seemed like the best way to get his bills paid. In time.

I let this sink in. How much money? I won't ask what for.

Significant, he says. No way you could raise it. Even I couldn't; I tried. He was—

Desperate. I do know. So, you both volunteered me. Sam gets out of trouble. I get taken for a ride. And the princess? What does she get?

Her money's worth. He laughs. This is, believe it or not, her show.

Victoria Anne is a terrorist? For *Ireland*?

Not bloody likely. She's a mixed-up kid who hates her family. This happens to make her interesting to many people a princess wouldn't ordinarily meet.

People who kill people.

His smile is just slightly condescending. Hardly the first of her kind, he says. Great Uncle Henry VIII was no slouch. Elizabeth I did it to her nice cousin Mary. There was a time a royal tot got no pudding till she learned to say "off with their heads." So now you know almost as much as I do. Would you mind helping me clean up this mess your pal Mutch left? I do believe we have one bottle still intact. Luckily it's the Cristal.

He pops the cork, pours, begins to hang up his suits and ties.

I sit there, numb.

He pauses with three hangers, an armload of shirts. Say *some*thing.

Is she the one with fringes?

He won't answer that. Just keeps tenderly folding his clothes, soothing them like hurt children.

We've got things to do, he mutters.

Right. Got to rescue drowning shirts. And kill the bad guys. Or the good guys? I keep forgetting.

God, I hate your sarcasm, he says. He offers me his glass. I don't touch it.

Hate my sarcasm, I echo. And what is it you like? What *was* it?

All the rest. You do know. He's got this angel-child look on. Baroque putto.

He parts with the stemmed goblet, pulls me toward him. Awkward pause. We're strange now, incapable of closing the space. I hate it that his slightest touch warms my blood; that he knows. I am trying not to lean into him. He knows this too. Darling, he begins. Then I see he's glancing at his wrist. At Sam's watch. I recover.

Oh, and could I have that watch back? It's the only thing my father left us to remember him by, apart from the debts.

I'm proud to say this surprises him. Of course it also tickles him, which unfortunately still excites me. I am a long way from immune.

Fancy a drive? he says. I can only nod my head yes, like a Chinese wooden doll. I fancy. I do.

The passenger seat is inexplicably missing; in its place, two plump cushions, gold-and-pumpkin silk with tasseled corners. Seated on these, I am considerably lower than usual; my eyes barely level with the dashboard. Unsafe at any speed. I don't ask what happened to the seat; I'm not up for another lie just now.

Where to? he says as he buckles me, none too securely, in. I have no reply to that; it was not a serious question.

His music swells; by now my body's liquid response is instant; Pavlov would be proud to have me in the lab. Some boy is singing about our lives coming between us.

He flashes his high-beam smile. Happy? he shouts. I can't believe my answer. It's yes.

Princess Victoria is nowhere, and therefore everywhere. I keep seeing her just ahead, there, taking the corner on two wheels, steering expertly into a skid. Her car is red, silver like ours, white; it's the Crusader; it's a TR-6, British racing green. She signals with her hand (the car's directionals aren't working); skeins of girlish laughter raveling from her deep purple sleeve.

Ludo absently mentions that I am not the first to ride beside him like this, minus a passenger seat, perched high instead on silken cushions, flying down unapproved midnight roads.

I can see her bright streaming hair, her head cocked at an arrogant angle, twisting to watch the mud of their wheels spatter the lads cheering from the hedgerows. Lads would cheer, never mind who the hell she was, the cheek of her, kicking up good Irish sod and muddying the issue.

Where was I when they were taking that last stretch of Corkscrew Hill, doing 90, 105, daring the devil? What caused the rev counter to stop counting? The windshield wiper to quit wiping? He's reaching around to do the job with his hand, something in his hand. Old Irish remedy, he says. It's a cut raw potato. Makes it sheer, he explains. A thousand uses for the Irish potato. This has been one of them.

Wherever they went, I fear, is where we are going now. And she is there, waiting.

Victoria, naughtiest member of her scandal-ridden royal generation, subject of rude graffiti since her tenth birthday. I remember, God help me. Her older brother, George, found an equerry in her bed and insisted on joining them. Vicky's dickies.

From then on she gave them something to scrawl about.

There was a West Indian stable groom, a math tutor, a school chum (female). Spending sprees and substance abuse, bingeing and whingeing. A tattoo: God Save my Mum, I Mean Bum, photographed by zoom lens in a ski resort sauna. (She was allegedly asleep, facedown.)

And finally, six months ago, the incident of the Queen's butterfly. A diamond-and-ruby Indian brooch. It went missing during a weekend house party in Vicky's flat at Balmoral Castle. The piece was not an official crown jewel, but it happened to be a favorite of the Queen's, a gift from an Indian prince to Vicky's great-grandmother, before her marriage to the then prince of Wales.

News of the theft was never made public. Staff were questioned, and Scotland Yard opened a confidential file on all of Vicky's houseguests. The brooch never surfaced. When some eagle-eyed royal watcher wondered in print why Her Majesty never seemed to wear it anymore ("Poor Butterfly?"), a copy was made from photographs, and on opening day at Ascot it appeared on her shoulder.

That was when Victoria Anne's behavior officially ceased to be a private worry. But the gravity of the government's concern was not made public either. An increased number of minders began to accompany her, to her pubs and parties; spas, beach resorts, trekking holidays. Some of these nannies were unknown to the princess herself. They were invariably young and pretty, boys or girls who hung out at her health clubs, her nightclubs; they stayed at her favorite hotels, traveled with her favorite rock bands.

For a while it even looked as though the V problem was under control.

They hadn't factored in Ludo. Now, speeding along this moonlit road, he tells me about it.

Despite his presence at Balmoral during the Poor Butterfly weekend, Scotland Yard had no real file on him. Partly because he was a famous rally driver, but mostly because he and his co-driver, an American diplomat's daughter, had only stopped at Balmoral for tea. A perfunctory check of his background revealed reassuring details. Proper aristo father, American mother, excellent schooling, impeccable connections, gently reared. Good credit rating. No perceptible politics or other suspicious habits. For good measure, the girl had just been presented at court. And since they hadn't stayed overnight it was assumed they'd had no chance to net the butterfly. Its loss was discovered two days later.

At the time, no one imagined that Vicky herself might have served it up in the drawing room, covered in clotted cream and popped inside a currant scone. Nor could anyone have guessed that its proceeds had been lodged in an Andorra bank. The account held funds for international traders in antiquities, arms, and, increasingly since the end of the cold war, weapons-grade radioactive alloys. Nuclear smugglers. Oh, that princess. That Vicky.

Preposterous; this foggy midnight run to meet a royal gun moll in dank crimson robes, ermine tails, diamonds on the butt of her Uzi.

As preposterous as my certainty, only yesterday, that Ludo was her assassin.

He's missed a turn; I hold my breath while he executes a

perfect 180-degree about-face, in reverse, without slowing down. It's a metaphor.

He finds the road: scenic route, a sliver of tar along the coast.

I decide to study my rally map, with the pinpoint of light from my pocket flash. Hopeless.

Turn that off, he says. We're there, anyway. Just about. Yes.

The road has turned nasty, one of those bleak, forgotten stretches that never rates county money for repairs. Wrecked car parts lie rusting in the fields on both sides. The headlight picks up a doorless Morris Traveler, filled with hay and squealing puppies.

Straight ahead, looming darker than the moonless sky, a great stone house on a steep rise, the only structure between the road and the sea. It's long and low, hugging the ground. Six ornate chimney stacks with little flaring four-cornered caps, like jester's crowns. Broken stone columns flanking a ruined gate that yawns into a courtyard choked with weeds and mud. This is the back of the house; its front faces a jagged sea cliff, and the sea itself, crashing against stone, answering the constant wind with desperate sighing.

There are lights on, giving the place no life, but somehow deepening the blackness of its vast bulk. Old Irish houses tend to look like children's drawings: squat, neat, two stories high, windows and door as symmetrical as the features of a plain, cheerful mother's face.

This sorrowful monster crept along its rocky promontory like the hull of a stone ghost ship run aground. It looked to be the age and design of the old British Coast Guard stations, abandoned in the 1920s but standing their lofty ground despite Irish independence. Lookouts kept vigil in these buildings during what the Irish still call "the emergency"—World War II. Which side they kept vigil for is not much talked about in the history books.

We're expected, Ludo says, steering sharply into the courtyard. I don't bother to ask by whom. There are two other parked cars, neither of them vintage. One has no license plate—just a number carefully written on the boot by a wet finger in caked dust. They must write it again after every rain.

We are met at the door by a shortish bearded man whose jaunty blazer is a size too small for his paunch. Nevertheless he has relentlessly fastened all its straining brass buttons, as though daring them to pop.

His accent seems proper Brit, what they call "received standard," but somehow I know he's what Ludo would regard as N.O.S.D. (not our sort, dear). Possibly a transplanted Yank. With airs. The blazer gives him away. Still, I like the shape of his head.

He leads us down a stone corridor that runs the full length of the house. Years of damp cold penetrate boots, socks, flesh, bones. At the end there are voices, light, the crackle of a wood fire. Ordinary party noises; somehow not reassuring. The little room, when we get there, seems too full. Enormous chairs drawn too close to the fire. A heavy mantel of carved marble, wonderfully out of place. What sort of nineteenth-century Irish farmer could have put it here?

Conversation dies as we approach; faces turn. Three men, one an elderly priest. And two women, one young and pale, crowned with a bush of copper-wire hair, like a terrier. The other older, rounder, olive-skinned, possibly Indian. She comes toward me, bright-eyed but unsmiling. None of them is smiling. I'm Chit, she says. Short for Chitra. You've met Sean. He's lovely, isn't he? Indicating the tight blazer. Chit, I echo, pronouncing it with care.

These are everyone else, she says with an airy wave. I nod again. They stare, then turn away quickly, as though something unpleasant has occurred, and they have agreed to ignore it. Thirty-seven witnesses do nothing while rape victim screams and dies. I. G. Farben executives negotiate calmly with Nazis as shots ring out in factory courtyard.

During a hostile takeover, nobody flinches.

Ludo disappears down that corridor with the lovely Sean. Each is armed with a double Irish in a fine crystal tumbler. I am not asked whether I'd like anything. Beyond the window empty fields turn their shoulders from the churning sea. Lights flicker in blurred clusters across the bay, little reminders of other life forms, towns, galaxies, far away.

The wire-haired woman has cornered the old priest and is telling him her childhood hurts, like rosary beads. Every week, she says, my sisters and I rehearsed our confessions. We dared not go in with nothing to declare. My sister Moira always had the best sins. Then came Denise, and Noreen. I was always desperate. One time—she giggles, leaning toward him. The priest recoils, reestablishing the appropriate distance.

Her voice drops. One time—

I strain to hear.

—I actually confessed that I'd made tea for my father, *unwillingly*.

The priest's expression remains benign. I notice his clerical collar is grimy; his black suit shines with neglect. He doesn't quite understand the woman's story, or that her foolish piety could make her laugh, now. Possibly he is considering what penance he would have exacted.

She backs away with a little sigh. Clearly she has now committed another sin, in confessing to him. This time perhaps unpardonable.

Panicking, she darts toward Chitra, the plump Indian lady, who isn't a bit pleased to see her coming. The men have gathered in tight knots, exchanging urgent whispers, shaking heads, scribbling on crumpled bits of paper. I can read fairly well upside-down, but the pencil stubs move so fast that all I can pick up is some factory beginning with Harr—.

I consider exploring the house, but as soon as I edge toward the doorway, the wire-haired woman and two of the men are all around me. It's like those secret electric fences for dogs. The pet's collar emits a mild shock as he approaches a no-go area; intensity increases as he moves closer to the invisible barrier. Unapproved road!

Can we get you something?

I was— I retreat instead to the window seat, just as Ludo returns with another full glass, or maybe it's the same one.

All right? he asks the men anxiously, like a guilty prom

escort who has ditched his ugly date. He shouldn't have brought her, the look says. His family made him.

I've got it, he whispers to me with sudden excitement. We're off.

Without thanking the host?

In the *car*, he says. Right now.

He's pulling me, and I trip trying to keep up. There's Sean staggering across the hall, at the far end. He's holding a towel to his face. Blue and white checks. I need to see more. Ludo tugs harder on my arm.

You're hurting.

Move, he says, not letting go.

But— And I twist for one last peek. The face above the blazer is striped with gashes. Blood running into the checkered cloth, dyeing the white squares. It's now a tartan. And Sean is no longer lovely.

We're safely strapped and doing 80, pothole jumping; a scary amusement park ride. I don't mention Sean. Instead I say: Tell me about the race you did last year.

Which one—the Alps? Monaco?

Tashkent to Istanbul.

That wasn't a race. Pleasure trip. Six beautiful cars, although Charlie Baker's Benz got confiscated at the Aralik border. Poor old Charlie forgot to bring a note from his ex-wife. The car was still in her name.

Aralik. Kars province. No pun intended. I remember— that's what you wrote on the postcard. I pause here, carefully; this territory is heavily mined. Wasn't that where they arrested some German art dealer and those Spanish guys? For smuggling. Not drugs. I read—

He shoots me an amused sidelong glance. Radioactives. It was a hoax, though. Stuff was planted by the German feds. Just to make a point about how easy it is. The guys were just businessmen with a cash-flow problem.

Oh. So how easy is it?

He holds up two fingers for me to supply with a lit cigarette. And to stop this line of questioning. He pops in a new cassette, too. Some girl wondering if God might be one of us. I notice he's got something in his other hand; it's the double shot of Irish whiskey. In the cut-crystal tumbler. Nice touch.

So, I say, are we going to the hotel? Do I get breakfast?

He floors the pedal, grinning. I suck in my breath. If he crashes us now, I can stop worrying about whether we're carrying plutonium. And whether he thinks that's what I think.

Well, who were those people? I have to shout over the girl singer's reassurance that God is great. Why did you bring me there?

Friends of friends, he shouts back. As I recall, you were in the mood. And they wanted to meet you.

I'm sure. Sean and Chitra. That old priest. Not forgetting the wire-haired terrier bitch. Dying to meet me.

Sean's a nasty piece of work, I admit. Your corporate empire grosses a billion a year, you tend to gross out the whole human race. As for poor old Father McGurk: altar boys. The usual. When the church put him out, he founded an open-air mission in a California redwood forest. *Giant* redwoods.

He takes his hands off the wheel to emphasize the point, then checks to see if I'm laughing yet. I'm trying not to.

And, he goes on, I don't know about the wire-hair. Unless she's working for Sean.

Would that be why Chit slashed his lovely face?

Who said she did? Almost anybody would. We're—here. We screech into the car park. Ten minutes. Just.

I'll collect the gear, he says. Oh, and the passenger seat. I had that rip repaired. Two rips. He pauses, while I remember poking holes in the seat. Then he adds: You check us out. And I'll have a couple of sticky buns.

Ah, Ludo, I'm sure you will.

He looks disgusted. I know I deserve it.

There's a message at the desk. It's for him, but I rip it open. No shame. Purple ink. Hotel stationery. Not this hotel. Where the hell were you? it says. Bastard. It's signed, V.

I pay the bill. By the way, I ask the clerk, waving the message; how far is this hotel from here?

The clerk points his chin toward the front door. Just opposite. They'll be starting the shoot momentarily.

The—shoot. I peer out the front door. Caravans and cars backed up in the driveway and parked all along the road. Swanky-looking tourists toting brand-new rifles. Americans, by the look of them. Shooting what? I say.

Pheasants. The clerk jerks his chin once more. Look, here they come.

As I watch, drivers open the doors of three vans. Flocks of pheasants hop out, onto the lawn, blinking at the weak morning sun. Not one takes wing.

All around me hotel guests rush to the windows; across the street, too, the windows are filled with excited spectators.

The tourists take aim and fire. Again; again. In minutes it's over. Hundreds of birds slaughtered, blood splattering the white gravel of the courtyard. Gillies with canvas bags rush out to clear away corpses, count them, and store them in the hotel freezer for the sportsmen.

I can't believe what I've witnessed.

Americans, mutters a fellow guest with obvious disdain.

Why didn't they fly? Why weren't they frightened?

They're hand-reared, says the guest. He's a Brit, accustomed to shooting birds in the air. Poor buggers, he says. They never learn to distrust people.

American sportsmen, the desk clerk explains, trying for a neutral tone, have only a day or two on business holidays. They expect to bag a dozen or so birds per shoot. Or they won't book again, d'you see. The Irish tourist board reckons the profit per bird is £1,000. Fair game, so. He chuckles.

I can't speak. I hand over a credit card, sign the bill. I'm an American, and I feel sick.

The gillies are still cleaning up, loading the body bags, as the gilded elevator door opens, and smiling Ludo appears. He has showered and changed. He looks gorgeous. Why is that?

I spring to attack. V wants to know where you were. To when does she refer? I proffer the message, and the ripped-open envelope.

This was addressed to me, he says coldly.

Opened by mistake. Sorry. I glance at the big clocks over the desk, which indicate the time in Paris, Frankfurt, New York . . .

Look, I say. We're late for time control. Three hundred penalty points!

He darts into the dining room, dashes back with a napkin full of buns and a look that says "don't jump salty with me," and hustles me toward the car park.

Let go, I say. Imperious tone. Let me *go*. He doesn't. A person called Enjoy rang, he says. She wonders if we know where Sam is.

My empty stomach lurches. Don't you know? Or are your friends making him walk around with some radioactive shit in his shirt?

Lord, you are an idiot, Ludo replies. I have to keep reminding myself that you're actually somebody's mother.

But not yours. I can't imagine anyone ever being yours.

Nobody was. His laugh is forced and harsh; it sets the suede fringes in riotous motion. And we're off. Roaring, exultant. Our last perfect day together. Ludo? Whatever happens, I'll never see you again. Ever. For reasons I don't want to fathom, I am welling up.

He sighs. I'll always be here.

I can tell he's sighed this before, lots of times. He does look sad. Always be "here." Wherever here is. I won't ask.

F I V E

Enjoy Ocasio, newly arrived at London's Heathrow Airport, is being scrutineered by a grim-faced Immigration officer. Her passport bears none of the tattoos of a frequent international traveler. Enjoy hasn't left New York in five years, except for one visit to her dying grandmother in Belize. Still, at this moment, in this place, she arouses more than routine interest.

The bandaged hand, of course. It looks makeshift, none too clean. She's Hispanic; she's headed for Ireland, no address. Her landing card states the purpose of her trip is pleasure, but she seems to have the jitters. Eyes abnormally bright, could be drugs. Clothes too flimsy for the climate, the time of year. Her answers are also flimsy.

True, she's just had a bumpy seven-hour night flight in a charter full of nuns, restless babies, and teenage line-dancing teams from the American heartland. The line of her

fellow passengers stretches a full half mile along the vast ar-
rivals hall. Interrogations are painstakingly slow. Girls in
team jackets lie sprawled on the industrial carpet; even the
nuns doze impiously on their lumpy carry-on bags. The
line's sinuous form, shaped by stanchions and ropes, suggests a bloated snake shedding exotic skins: bright puffy
jackets, trailing baby-seat straps; duty-free sacks of silvery
plastic.

Enjoy carries nothing but a battered canvas backpack. She
has no baggage claim checks.

Backpackers do travel light in Ireland. European kids,
most of them, traveling by bus and ferry; hitching, crashing
in hostels, littering the pavements of Dublin and Galway,
busking or braiding each other's hair for pub money or the
fare home. This person does not fit that picture.

Possibly the officer wouldn't be quite so squinty-eyed if
there hadn't been the bombing at Newry, the tension around
the peace talks.

A delicate moment, this. Delicate.

How will you be traveling to Ireland? he asks her. Miss,
er, Ocasio? That's not O'Casey, I presume?

Car and boat. Not O'Casey, she says primly.

Long trip, eh? Long day's journey into night boat. Fishguard?

She nods. He jots this.

And then? How long in Ireland?

A week. Or so. Hitchhiking around.

Thought you were driving.

A friend is. Giving me a lift over. To, uh, Rosslare.

Uh-huh. Ferries go either Fishguard-Dun Laoghaire, or Holyhead-Rosslare. So which is it, then?

I guess Dun—that one.

He sets his mouth in a hard line, stamps the passport: Entry granted for 24 hours. Then he waves her through to Customs.

Ocasio, he jots on the notepad. Hispanic female, 24. Bandaged right hand.

At Heathrow, security is now even tighter at Customs than at the check-in gate. Detectors react to chemical substances as well as to metal. In recent months, chemicals have been traveling in ever more ingenious containers: a baby's soiled nappy, a menstruating woman's tampon; the belly of a prize standard poodle.

Any suitcase left unattended is destroyed within five minutes, after a single warning on the loudspeakers. Rubbish bins are checked by roving guards in cars equipped with beeping sensors. Outside on the runways, dogs meet all incoming flights, presniffing the cargo as it hits British soil.

So a bloody bandage is a red flag at Heathrow Customs. Enjoy's is carefully unwrapped on request. It reveals nothing but her wound, still oozing. The Red Hand of Ulster, mutters the inspector, signaling her to wrap it up, fast.

I was cleaning up, she volunteers. Some broken plates.

He hadn't bothered to ask. The call from Immigration has already come in.

By the time she boards her bus for Victoria Station, Ocasio, Hispanic female, 24, bandaged right hand, is being followed. She checks her reflection in her compact mirror, slowly repairs her lipstick, surveying her fellow passengers as they settle into their seats. There. That's the one. She permits herself a tiny sigh of relief. As Ludo would say, Who's a clever girl, then?

At Victoria Station, an elderly priest is waiting in a blue van, with the motor running. He's not wearing his clerical collar; just a black suit, with a Jesuit pin in the buttonhole.

Enjoy hops into the van without a backward glance. If the police are on her case, it's up to them to pay attention.

Father McGurk tries not to be distracted by his passenger's NEW F——ING YORK T-shirt, her black fingernails, her iridescent mouth. The filthy bandage, however, he feels free to notice. Ought to have that looked at, he grumbles. When we get there.

Is it far? she says, to be sociable.

Oh, quite. Eight hours, anyway. And then the wait for our boat. Three forty-five in the ayem, is when it goes.

Some ungodly hour, Enjoy says with a nervous giggle. Daring a little joke at his expense. Will Sam—? But she changes her mind. Will anyone meet us?

Shouldn't think so, till we're there. We are on our separate journeys, know what I mean?

London streetlights blur in the rain as they sputter through traffic, retracing the path she has just traveled by bus. Out of town, past the airport. Her head droops, her eyes close. The priest turns onto the motorway heading north for Holyhead, not south for Fishguard.

From the unmarked gray sedan six cars behind them, this detail is duly forwarded to London, Dublin, and Belfast.

Sam, wearing a three-piece suit, hair slicked back in a corporate ponytail, has already landed in Ireland. He carries a glossy leather briefcase. Despite the sore jaw, his smile is easy; he radiates cool. On his landing card, he mentions he will be staying at Kyteler Manor, the Westmeath estate of Sean Harrison, Ireland's foremost entrepreneurial genius. His international holdings range from liquor, food, and soft-drink companies to resort hotels and phone services for sex, prayer, and tax shelters. Sam's ticket on this flight was hastily arranged by Sean Harrison's travel office, marked highest priority, because Sam is a member of the wedding. This Sunday, Harrison's daughter Majella is getting married to Charlie Baker, one of Ludo's rally-driving buddies, who roomed with Ludo and Sam at Yale.

Only last month Sam had sent his regrets; no way he could raise the fare. Then, presto! Night before last, things changed. Charlie was delighted, though there are now thirteen ushers, counting the groom's black-sheep first cousin, who had to be flown in from Argentina as Sam's replacement.

Of course, they're still expecting Ludo. He'll finish his rally just in time. He'll miss the bachelor dinner and probably the rehearsal. But he'll make the ceremony. Looking gorgeous. Charlie understands perfectly.

For months, tabloids on both sides of the Irish Sea have

feasted on this all-but-royal wedding. Brilliant Brit Romeo and his carrot-top colleen of a Juliet.

It's no accident that the event at Kyteler Manor coincides with the Anglo-Irish summit just a few miles away. Most of the delegates, business cronies of Sean Harrison's at one time or another, will take time out to attend the reception. Harrison's invitations are rarely declined by anyone doing business in Ireland.

At Shannon, Sam is whisked through Immigration and Customs without so much as a rude question. Front-line soldiers in the tourism industry do roll out the emerald carpet for the rich, the famous, and anyone who seems to be on their A-list. Ireland of the thousand welcomes.

A customer relations man escorts Sam to his waiting limousine, helps load his suitcases into the boot. They're heavy, for a weekend visit. Invitations to Kyteler Manor tend to involve a fair number of wardrobe changes: white dinner jackets and black; kilts if you're entitled to them; sporting togs for croquet, angling, riding; sweaters for spins in sports cars; Wellies for tramps in soggy woods. Not to mention topper and morning coat for the actual wedding.

Even the tony British press, which normally snubs anything Irish as somewhat low-rent, have taken this particular romance to their frosty hearts. Possibly because of the timing. Charlie and Majella have come to symbolize the peace process, much as Europe's royal intermarriages used to do in the old days.

So every detail has been worth a page-one photo; a closing tidbit for the evening news. Belfast lace to trim the veil!

What price the groom's damask waistcoat? What would London hairstylists do with Majella's bush of wild Irish hair? And wasn't it grand that the page boys had venerable titles, while the flower girls had names like Attracta and Assumpta?

Even the custom-designed portable toilets, shipped by ferry, made the media. The gold basin taps, the faux naughty etchings on the walls. Fifteen hundred guests expected. So, as one headline writer quipped, Does the pope go in the woods?

In fact, there will be a special ceremony in the woods, as well as one in a tent. Two clerics officiating, Church of England in the tent, and an old family friend, Father Desmond McGurk, conducting an outdoor service amongst the ancient pine trees.

Wedding consultants thoughtfully providing a thousand umbrellas.

In the limousine, Sam fidgets with the electronic toys, appraises the crystal-and-silver fittings on the drinks tray, checks the champagne in the minifridge. Roasted pecans, Havana cigars, toilet kits with stuff for eyes, ears, nose, throat, hair, teeth, shoes, and attitude. He considers the phone and fax. No one to call. In all of the real world, no one to call. He sighs, activates the shiatsu massager in his seat back. Leather-sheathed bumps pulse and thrum on the nape of his neck, down his spine. The leather sighs as it moves, decidedly weird. He wonders if the engineers threw that in for laughs. What if the car were filled with businessmen? Five suits getting off on this at once. The ultimate safe orgy. True glove.

Reposing on the front seat beside the driver is a large square parcel, the last item packed in the car by the helpful customer relations man. Tag on it is addressed to Sean Harrison's New York office. Sam cranes to decipher the sender's scrawl: Ludo.

Last-minute wedding gifts, eh? he ventures. The aide closes the subject with a firm slam of the door and a brisk wave. The driver touches his cap in lieu of a reply.

From the outside, Father McGurk's van is like any other in Ireland, where you get a tax break for choosing a big car you can't see out the sides of, or carry more than one passenger in. The blindsided van is a cargo vehicle, unsafe to operate and very popular.

Father McGurk has a red velvet curtain behind the front seat, which renders his cargo invisible. From time to time, when he swerves, the curtain slides open, as though to reveal the Wizard of Oz working his dubious magic. So Enjoy catches a glimpse of the secrets behind her. Fitted shelves and cubbyholes line the walls from floor to roof; plastic boxes containing nuts, bolts, washers, screws, boot hinges, all neatly labeled. Pieces of hollow tubing, elbow joints, sheets of metal, cut to size and marked. Tools with their outlines precisely drawn to show precisely where they hang. The van is a mobile garage, an auto parts shop.

You tinker with cars, Father? she asks.

The word tinker, he says, is politically incorrect in Ireland. But yes, I do.

For yourself, or for other people?

Mostly as a hobby. Though I rebuilt a Princess once. One of those big high-top saloons. Friend of mine keeps it parked outside his pub, as an extra snug, like. You sit in it and have a few jars, while you wait to get inside.

Mm. You don't have a radio? It's okay; I brought my Walkman. She rummages in her backpack, plugs in. Father McGurk drives on, alone with his thoughts. Oxford, Cheltenham, the Cumbrian Mountains. They reach the coast with four hours to spare, before they'll be permitted to drive onto the boat.

Holyhead is literally a bedroom community serving the ferry lines; the shore littered with dreary bed-and-breakfasts for exhausted travelers with no place to go.

We'll stay in one of these, McGurk says. It's ten quid. Including a breakfast we won't want. Coffee on the boat. I'll knock when it's time. See to that bandage if I were you.

This time tomorrow, sighs Ludo, Charlie Baker ties the knot. A hundred miles from here.

I know, I say. Little Lord Fauntleroy's second time around. And this time he strikes it richer.

Sam was supposed to come.

I don't know how to respond to this. But I gather Ludo still intends to make it. You're going, then?

Of course. We'll finish in time. Okay with you?

Oh, sure. Just drop me off one of these Kerry mountains, I'll get a cab.

But you're coming with me. He looks startled, as though we had an understanding.

You *are* coming? he says again. Charlie's expecting you—as Sam's—

Mother.

Representative. I mean you're here, and he's not.

I've never met Charlie. I wasn't invited. I have nothing to wear.

He laughs. You'll meet him. You're invited with me. You'll wear whatever you're wearing. A glance at my damp Irish sweater, my mud-caked Wellies. Well, you'll change.

My brain suddenly clicks on. When did you tell them about me?

Tell who what?

Charlie and his fancy new relations. That I was . . . with you.

Don't recall. Yes, I do. As soon as you said you'd be my co-driver. I told them, they said to bring you, of course. Sean's like that. He's got a wedding to do, he'll do parties nonstop, the whole weekend. Invite the world. It's cost-effective. The world drinks your excellent champers Sunday, can they say no to you Monday? About anything? And in any case you have met them. At the house. Sean? And Chit?

Thought you said *he* was a shit, too.

Did I? Never mind. There'll be a thousand guests, at least; I promised you'd behave yourself. And your place card—with the 3-D etching of Kyteler Manor, and your name in twenty-four-karat gold calligraphy—is all done up. Ireland's most coveted souvenir.

Apart from a Harrison bride of your own? I say that just because. Who slashed his face, then? I add.

No response to these. Look, he says instead, sounding put out. I need you there, full stop. Then he softens it, touches my hair, lets his fingers rest there. We'll have been through so much. Survived this rally. Please stay with me.

I have time to ponder it all as we move into the line-up for test number fifteen. CAUTION! the sign warns. I know; I know.

The rain is blowing sideways again. Navigators who have umbrellas open them as they climb out. Ludo needs one fast look at the diagram. It's a hieroglyph shaped like a uterine device, triangular, with a factory at the right corner. Harrison Chemical Factory. Rings a bell: Harr—.

The start is a squiggle, the middle goes straight to the factory wall, then doubles back into a quadruple-curve reverse spiral.

He nods, shoves the paper into my hand. Start official signals go, and he roars off. The TV cameras are on him. So is mine. For the record: silver mist on silver car, his wet hair streaking across his brow as he swerves, cutting in close to the markers, speeding into reverse, taking the corners like a skater, gliding, claiming all the ice behind him.

Brilliant, I think, as he stops on a dime, straddling the lines. Neat. One last pylon wobbles, he might have cut it too fine, but it stays upright. Five-mark penalty, max.

I run through the rain to meet his smile; he's scowling. Timing too slow. Zan would beat it. Mutch too. Hell, even the Reliant girls. Not fast enough. Not perfect. He likes his performances to be perfect.

Enjoy is awake when Father McGurk raps on her door. She's hardly slept, staring instead at the walls, at cheerful pictures of children on a sunny beach. There's a shower in the corner. One-night tourists can always find a shower in the corner. Enjoy's hand is throbbing, though. Better not to get it wet. Better to stretch out instead, carefully, on top of the covers, and follow the darkness with half-closed eyes. Questions throbbed in her mind like the pulsing of pain in the hand.

Where was Sam? What was this place? Sam said she had to come here because of what happened. She would not be safe in New York. He would not forgive himself if harm came to her there because of him.

People knew how she'd helped him; how Hernando happened to go downstairs for the pizza; why he never came back.

I can take care of myself, she argued. Defiant Latina far from home. But even she didn't believe it. How could she have stayed at Sam's place, or her own place, or Hernando's? Those seemed to be all the choices.

Until Sam told her what they could do, what they must do. It would be all right, he'd fix everything. They'd be together, they'd be safe. Ireland, he said. They must go to Ireland, he knew a way to get the money. They must fly separately, then meet. Ludo would be there to help them. No matter what.

So unlike Sam to be so calm, so sure. The phone call to Ludo, what to say, and another call Sam would make to some rich old *cabrón* they knew over there; with a daughter who was getting married. Somehow he would put it all together—the tickets, everything. And she was still too numb to ask questions. Hernando was dead. Hernando had a gun, and cut her, and tied them both up. She made a phone call, for pizza. Not for pizza. These things belonged in a movie. One of those where Enjoy would have hidden her eyes, or gone to the ladies' room till it was over.

Who would take care of Sam's cats if they left? She did ask that. He promised to arrange this too. He promised.

Now she lay here staring at the dank ugly room in this "holy head." How could they give this name to such a place? She lay here thinking, Sam lied, there was no one to feed the cats. If he could lie in this, he would lie also about other things.

And this old priest with the car full of screws and pipes. Taking her to someplace, who could tell where. No one knew where she was, even now. Enjoy Ocasio, real name María Luz Encarnita Ocasio y Figueroa, age twenty-four. So she lay very still as silent tears slid out of her eyes and into her hair, into her ears with the little gold hoops, onto the hard rubber pillow and the bed with pink ruffles. She sang to herself and played her music in the earphones. She felt the throbbing of her wounded hand. What had the Customs man called it? Ulster's Red Hand. On the boat she will ask the priest what it means. She will ask at least this.

SIX

Sean Harrison always has a lot of balls in the air. He has come far since his desperate days as a lad in Tuam, that rude western town on the N17. Desperate. Could throw a ball, however. Could catch too, and run like hell, and come up smiling from a pileup. He played all the games there were—soccer, Gaelic football, tennis. His drunken da never had any use for him except when he scored in the games. And then there were girls. Sean was fierce handsome, they said, though girls were a bit like Da, no use for you unless you scored in the games. His and theirs. He learned well. Played every point as if life depended on it, and so it did. Got his good-looking mug constantly in the sports pages, made his da a hero in the pub, if not in the family.

And then, so the Harrison legend went, Sean's richAmerican uncle took a fancy to the lad and brought him to the States for schooling. "RichAmerican" was always just the one word in Ireland, especially for emigrant Irishmen who made good "over there." Sean's uncle Jacky had made very good. It was said that he did dark deeds for Kennedys long before a plaster head of JFK was set on every Irish mantel shelf, next to the pope himself. Whatever Sean Harrison's uncle had to do to make his fortune mattered far less back home than the fortune. So when Jacky offered to take the boy and train him to be a richAmerican, too, the local footballers wept in the pub, but the family was glad to see the back of him.

Growing up in Boston at his uncle's business and political knee, Sean learned a whole new ball game. He was a natural—brains enough, blarney to spare, and Irish eyes that smiled when they had something to hide.

So it must have come as a shock to the hometown folks when Sean's uncle Jacky was indicted in the U.S. on Federal charges of tax fraud and money laundering, just as Sean slid silently back to the West of Ireland. Luckily he was by then a richAmerican, considerably richer than Jacky. And still smiling as he came out of the pileup.

Over the years there were persistent rumors in the U.S. that Sean might have set Jacky up, that he was in charge of the dark deeds, and that when the Feds came sniffing around, Sean had hollered Uncle, taken the money and run.

Jacky pleaded guilty to things that put a dent in his fortune but kept him out of jail. And Sean became head of Jacky's business empire, based in Ireland but expanding nicely everywhere.

Even I had read how he shed his wives with expensive

Vatican annulments, and that he had met the latest one, a plump Pakistani heiress, in a VIP lounge at London's Heathrow Airport. She of course would be Chitra the slasher, who described herself in interviews as "tinted." Harrison-watchers were fond of counting their joint holdings: houses in the States, castles in Ireland, flats in London, Frankfurt, and Geneva. A marina in West Cork, where, coincidentally, drugs came in to Ireland for the European market—and a shipping line based in the North Sea, where, coincidentally, matériel went out to the Middle East arms industry.

If any Irish company had a problem, there was by now only one surefire solution. In the old days you'd have heard the name Guinness mentioned, and later Smurfit or O'Reilly. Now it was "Can we get Harrison in on this? Can we get Sean to just put in a word?"

He was credited with settling the transit strike, and bringing two banks back from the brink. It was said he had managed to get a regional airport built with money from the Vatican and the CIA, so the Yanks could always use Ireland as a fuel stop for fighter jets on their way to start a war in the Third World—if not a third World War.

People who worked for him, he had said, had to learn the art of the possible—to apply to the impossible. He did not say that big favors were done for dangerous people, who understood that bigger favors would be exacted later in return. This was, according to Ludo, one of the many moves Sean had learned from his uncle Jacky.

No one could tell you much about his politics. In interviews, and to his biographers, he would say that the Jesuits had taught him right, sports had taught him winning, and life had taught him the necessary.

Inevitably, enemies called him a shamrogue. Defenders retorted that he was surely a rogue, but never a sham.

Needless to say, his accountants approved of everything he did—up to and including the latest marriage. Tough for the Irish to earn the odd crust these days—even if your name is Harrison.

They might be joking. But when Irishmen joke they're dead serious. His soft-drink company was going belly-up. His regional airport was seeking a merger to bail it out. Even his woollen mill, Ireland's pride, was closing a deal with a factory in the former Yugoslavia. Cheaper labor, a shoddier product, and another three hundred Irishmen on the dole. Workers at the home plant in Donegal threatened to walk out—until Sean announced he'd close shop altogether.

Meanwhile, if Ludo was to be believed, Sean's people in the States were being persuaded to do some favors that were very dark indeed. Deals, moves, and the unseen hand of old uncle Jacky calling in markers. None of this would make the papers. All of it was more in the political line than Sean was used to. But he was still a quick study. And now he had a very rich wife. She, too, had been taught right, winning, and necessary.

From the moment the *Faerie Queen* docked, Father McGurk began having car trouble. You would think he could handle anything along those lines, what with that arsenal of bits and pieces behind the red curtain.

He could jump-start the van all right, and they'd go for a kilometer or two. Then they'd stall out again. It took two hours to make the town of Kilcock, a twenty-minute distance from the ferry slip, even counting Dublin's morning traffic.

At this rate they'd be all day. And Father McGurk didn't have all day. He needed to deliver his cargo—including Enjoy Ocasio—to a certain location at a certain time. People were depending on him. Indeed, if he could be permitted a slight immodesty, just shy of the deadly sin of pride, history was depending on him.

Every time they stopped, someone tried to help. Urchins with borrowed jumper cables, tinkers with ulterior motives, farmers with tractors, *gardai* with puzzled expressions. There was even a *garda* who had known Father McGurk in County Sligo years ago, when the priest had found him loitering with intent outside a walled apple orchard. The officer recalled the moment with some relish. Would you ever climb over that wall to steal an apple? the priest had demanded. The frightened lad replied, No, Father, I'd never.

And Father McGurk, with a twinkle in his holy eye, whispered, Not even for me?

At which the youth had scampered up the crumbling twenty-foot stone wall, packed his shirt with a dozen of the best, and clambered back down, ripping his trousers, skinning both knees.

The priest accepted the boy's tribute of forbidden fruit—every last apple—and exacted ten Hail Marys from him the following Sunday. Later he exacted certain other favors, too. The boy never told anyone. When the scandal broke and Father McGurk went off to America, the boy was a man. He wept for the vindication and never went back to church.

Now that boy was here, up against the window of the blue van, leering over at Enjoy Ocasio, inquiring: How can I help, Father?

Considering what else was in the van, the priest hesitated. Then he said softly: Bless you, my son. We could do with a push, surely.

It was dark when they arrived, with a new starter motor, at the house that crept like a great stone beast alongside the boiling sea.

The wind was fierce, rain and hail blowing sideways, lights and phones out for miles.

Not such an unusual night along this desolate coast road. But to Enjoy, daughter of a hot, still country, toughened only by a few mean streets in New York's cold heart, this seemed the howling end of the world.

Judging from the priest's tense mood, she could have been right. As they entered the muddy courtyard, he ordered her out of the van, never mind the downpour, or the fact that only candles flickered dimly from inside the house. No one came to the door. He turned the van and stopped with his front wheels facing the gate, poised for a quick getaway.

As she climbed out, a swinging stable door blew off its single rusted hinge, and flew like some errant, lethal Frisbee, crash-landing three feet from where she stood.

The priest barely flinched; he had safely maneuvered the

van's back end to the steps of another crumbling outbuilding. Stony as a prison, with slits for windows, no railing for the outside stair, no sign of habitation. Pigeon loft, by the look of it.

Enjoy stood alone in this pelting hail, banging with her good fist on a little blue door, while the priest mounted those slippery steps, staggering under some mysterious burden he had removed from the back door of the van.

Sam? she shouted, though she knew that whatever there was inside this house, it wasn't likely to be Sam. Still, she cried his name, as though the sound itself had a power. Besides, there was nothing else to cry.

The priest was suddenly behind her; she jumped, cringing as though he would harm her. He barely touched the door and it flew open with the force of the wind. Luckily it swung in, and the two of them fell forward with it. McGurk here! shouted the priest. Bit of car trouble on the Dublin road. Are ye all gone, then?

A figure emerged from the shadowy corridor, flashing a torch. Given you up, barked a gruff voice from behind the light, which shone full on Enjoy, shivering in her once saucy costume. The beam traced her body, top to bottom, before the voice said, Come in to the fire, then, there's a cuppa, I'll find ye a blanket or something.

To the priest, he said only, Where is it?

Pigeon loft, McGurk replied. All set.

What about this one? A thumb jerked over his shoulder at the crumpled-up girl dripping into the sitting room fire.

McGurk raised his shoulders like a man of God submitting to his master's will. I was told nothing. Only to bring her here.

The other man offered an exasperated sigh.

Well, said McGurk. If you don't mind, I'll take a cuppa myself, then I'm gone. The rest will be back, I expect? I mean, we're here in good time, all things considered.

The other man led the way to the sitting room. There's a bit of ginger cake left. I'll fetch the girl some clothes. She can hang up her gear. What there is of it.

They were alone then, with their teacups to fill the silence.

When is Sam coming? She forced herself to ask this.

Can't be long, said the priest cheerfully. He was starting before we docked. You'll have a rest here and be on your way, the two of you. The others will see to anything you need. He gestured vaguely.

She looked at him hard in the flickering light. For the first time, really. And knew at once he was lying. Sam wasn't coming. Was never meant to come.

Please, she said softly. That was all.

But the priest had no time to hear it. His upraised hand ended its gesture in an awkward wave, and he fled into the teeming darkness.

Enjoy had no time either, as it turned out. The priest's van had scarcely clattered out of the yard and onto the road when another car screeched in. Suddenly there was a burst of shouting, and the barking of dogs; boots crunched over the gravel.

Enjoy began to run, screaming, down the endless corridor, toward the noise. Help! she cried. Somebody help!

The man with the flashlight was out in the yard, his hands raised over his head. There were other men, two or three, running down the steps of the pigeon loft, shouting curses. Flames spurted from inside the loft, signaling like frantic semaphores into the sky, changing hailstones into points of orange ice.

In the yard below, dogs tangled with men and tore free. A shot rang out; then another. Threads of fire began to seep through the narrow pigeon roost openings; tiny darting tongues seeking a quick taste of freedom.

From the door of the loft, two men struggled with heavy suitcases, trying to maneuver on the slippery stone landing. One stumbled on the first slick step; the second dropped his burden and edged past, scrambled down the steps around the building and up over the seawall. His abandoned luggage exploded at the same moment the slate roof gave way, collapsing inward, sending a column of bright smoke up into the storm.

Help me! cried Enjoy Ocasio, for the last time.

One of the guns in the yard answered her. As she fell, the tattered bandage came undone, streaming across her body like a white ribbon against the bursting light.

Figures scattered, pursued by shots. Some fell, others vanished. The rest, with their dogs and torches, sifted hastily through the wreckage. They found a sealed pickle jar, tossed it into their car, and sped off.

Two fields away, at the end of another road to the sea, a red sports car had been parked for an hour with its lights off. It was at a spot down at the edge of the cliffs, where a lone fisherman might try his luck in the daytime, or a pair of lovers at night. There was a No Dumping sign—warning picture of a little car topping over the cliff. And a small tourist board notice about the holy well nearby.

The little red car had been seen earlier by Paddy Clarke, who owned the general store and the Fiddler's Elbow, a pub on the main road.

Then, right after the explosion at the lodge, Paddy saw the car again, making its way back from the cliffs and onto the road, doing 75, maybe 80, in the opposite direction.

There are stretches of Irish coastline so desolate that a stranger's gaze finds nothing to rest upon, field after silent field.

But the Irish say that you can't do anything, anywhere in Ireland, that somebody doesn't see.

Zan is running dangerously late. That bloody fool of a priest barely made it out. Wouldn't have if the police van hadn't made a wrong turning off the coast road.

He'll have no time now to check the scene, or to chase the little coward who escaped over the wall. Hell, they'll scarcely make it back to the passage checkpoint before the rally officials close it. Three hundred penalty points if they skip the stop.

Giles suggests a bold shortcut, up and over the back of a sea cliff, approach the checkpoint from the other side. Instructions strictly forbid this, of course. Approach from N, leave toward SW, is what it says. So the maneuver will cost a few points. Hardly any, compared to missing it altogether.

Right, then. Zan floors the pedal. Halfway up to what the map calls One Man Pass, it's already clear: this is a mistake. How serious is clear fifty yards on. The path dwindles abruptly to a rock-strewn rut, formed by a stream swollen beyond its bounds by two days' heavy rain. It's no go, full stop.

Just as the ledge narrows, Zan tries a sharp twist of the wheel; possibly it's not too late to turn back. The rear tires sink deep and fast, spinning in mud, sinking deeper. One front wheel now hangs over the precipice, also spinning, but in thin air.

That tears it, Zan says. Done for.

Giles hops out in search of flat bits of wood, to slide under the back end. Maybe they can rock it free. There's nothing.

Are you effing daft? Zan yells. Go fetch a tractor. With a winch!

The winch is dead, Giles retorts. No time for jokes, however.

Move! you bastard. Zan is fuming now. Forget the checkpoint. We're sitting here, spitting distance from that fire, and the raid. What do you think the cops are doing? Even the Irish ones—

Giles is already out of earshot, plunging down the steep cliff road.

Princess Victoria Anne sighs and puts the top up, peels off her sopping Zan wig, wrings it, lets loose the bright cascade of her own hair, sinks back against the white leather headrest. A deceptive posture; inside she is doing 120, maximum performance level, up on two wheels in the turns.

She is pushing imaginary pins around the war-room map in her mind. Estimated situation: Priest, just about here. Red pin. Ludo, approximately there. Blue pin. The lodge, police raid, material planted for seizure, lab analysis, timing, diversion of military attention. So far, perfect. Areas outlined in black, yellow arrows to indicate direction of troops and matériel. Next point, where all pins converge: Kyteler Manor, Sunday. Harrison wedding. Sean, Chit, Ludo, and the priest. Volunteers, high-grade samples, customers/targets, life-and-death bargaining table—engraved place cards for all.

She permits herself a fleeting smile. Who else could have dreamed up so elegant a scenario? Who else could make it happen?

She no longer doubts that it will. What they're selling is too good to refuse. And if they don't buy, it's good enough to make them very, very sorry.

She ticks off the predictable outcome of no-sale: peace talks wrecked, heads of three nations, including the U.S.A., shaken, rattled, possibly rolled.

Best of all, the spectacle of her family. Scared Mama herself delivering her self-pitying speech on the BBC, in her warbling tremolo: My husband and I . . . are most distressed . . .

Meanwhile, war headlines: LOOSE NUKES!

Assuming the priest doesn't crash his van. And Ludo gets there without any wild Ludo plot twists at the critical moment. Always a risk with that boy. Useful, but erratic. Hates taking orders from a woman. Easily bored, too; attention span shortens after sex.

Which was why, Vicky told herself, she'd had to get involved with Sean Harrison. In spite of the paunch, the Irishness, and the dangerous wife. Though she did turn out to have a lovely family. Imagine! Karachi arms dealers. It was true, what everyone said about flying first class. Destiny is always in the next seat.

Now that she's had time to reflect, she'll admit that Sean is proving risky too. Never sleep with a man whose wife is too rich in her own right. Especially if she's handy with knives. Even a princess needs to zig and zag.

When she isn't sitting here, up to her favorite car's ass in a mud slide called One Man Pass.

She reaches into the glovebox for her sleek organizer with the royal crest embossed on every page. By appointment. She begins to make notes. Flowcharts. Diagrams. When she doodles, it's the international symbol for radioactive nuclear material.

Earliest time of arrival for Ludo: one hour before the indoor tent ceremony. McGurk's performance in the woods precedes. Materials in place two P.M. Parking lot attendant. Reception five.

Ludo's co-driver? Vicky pauses, frowning. The flashing gold pen hovers over the page. What do we know about her? More to the point, what do we know about her and Ludo? There's what he told us. We can discount that. And that they haven't done it. Bloody hell they haven't. She doesn't know the extent of her son's involvement. Well, that could be true. Ludo recruited her only because of the son. Believe that, I've got a ten-kiloton bomb to sell you.

Her face softens into another rare smile. After all, not even poor old Giles is here. Though he'd give something to see it.

In fact, what the hell is keeping him? She definitely saw a tractor just down that hill, in one of those scruffy farmyards. Though God knew whether there'd be petrol in it. These people.

Briefing points for Sean, she writes: Round up delegates early, with family. Pose for photos, wedding video. At which time our offer can be briefly outlined and circulated. *Library.*

Will Sean have formal presentation? Slides showing potential targets (with damage). Background: who we are, sources, asking price, conditions, guarantees . . .

Details of merchandise. She checks another page for the inventory. Reads like a recipe from Mrs. Beeton:

Plutonium, fifth of an ounce. Extraordinary purity. Test sample for analysis.

Uranium, one pellet. Highly enriched. Flown in fresh from Prague, via Munich.

Strontium 90, three capsules. Sealed containers.

Plus: Assorted bits and bobs small and light enough to pop into Jiffy bags and sent, separately, Federal Express, to desired locations. Alloy added for extra stability, no extra charge for handling. (Remind Sean: Friend of mine brought in 3/4 pound of plutonium, highly radioactive, on Lufthansa, Moscow to London, in a nice Louis Vuitton bag. Shame about the bag.)

V. important: we are *not* amateurs. One of our people recently stole plutonium from Obninsk weapons-design lab, stripped, showered, passed through detectors at military checkpoints. He said it was hardly the biggest thing he'd ever had up his bum.

Also: 1. We're not greedy. Check out details of last deal with Pakis. (Ask bride's charming stepmother!)

2. No junk. No slivers of p. from old Russian smoke detectors, like some people are peddling.

3. And there's more where these came from.

Finally, no deal, we make our own fireworks with what we have. Take out Buck Palace, Washington, New York, in one go. Our lads say if the rascals who did the World Trade Center had used a pinch of our powder, they could have put Wall Street out of commission for 10 years. Without exploding it.

Sean says we won't get 20 million (dollars). Even though it's what the Yanks paid the Kazakhs in '94. Of course that was a straight government deal. No middle men. *And* they got 200 weapons' worth.

Note from Mutch: Our lads want in on all future summits. They feel left out, like the Tomsk-7 physicist we just recruited. He used to be a hometown hero. Now he makes less than the char who sweeps the nuke rubbish in his old lab.

She snaps the organizer shut, glares out the streaked window, willing Giles to materialize. Seconds later, he does. Filthy sodding mess, riding high in a tractor cab with a strapping local lad. And wearing an idiotic, ecstatic grin, until he catches the scathing look on Vicky's face.

Still, fifteen minutes later, she has to forgive him. He and tractor boy balancing with a foot each over the cliff while they hook the vehicles. Then, later still, covered with even blacker mud that she churns in their faces as she rises from it, like Venus from the seabed.

They get the car hoisted, turned, and headed back the way they came an hour before. Zan is back in the driver's seat, not a silken tendril of hair out of place.

Halfway down, tractor boy climbs out, unhooks the Lotus, stands grinning at them in the pelting rain.

Zan signals to Giles: a fiver.

The fellow refuses, wipes his face with his filthy oilskin sleeve, and waves them on, with a You're all right!

Fancy that, says Zan. Giles can't help sighing. He does indeed fancy that.

S E V E N

~〜~

A pair of falcons, carved in stone, brood over the massive pillars flanking the front gate of Kyteler Manor. The driveway from this point to the house is fully two curving miles, thickly wooded on the river side, formally landscaped on the other. Sheep graze decoratively all along the way, never bothering to look up at passing cars. The scene is an eighteenth-century landscape painting by a minor nineteenth-century artist. British, of course.

At the gate lodge, a sentry greets the limousine driver, touching his cap with a one-finger salute. The backseat passenger, Sam, rates hardly a glance. The route from here is dotted with sleek parked cars, all pertaining to the family and those guests invited for the weekend. There are two immense spaces at the rear of the house roped off and divided by numbers, for tomorrow's invading army.

Gaily striped canopies are already in place, covering the

lawns, bracketed by the rose gardens, carefully angled so as not to obscure views of the house and, beyond it, the grand flight of two hundred steps leading down to the private wood. This forest of rare and ancient imported trees follows along the river's edge for several miles, looping back to the rear courtyard. There are secret follies hidden in the woods, to be found by venturesome guests: a horse monument, baroque, terrazzo, as intricately carved as a cathedral spire; a miniature Greek temple; the marble tombstone of a dog called Phizz, buried at the feet of his master, whose own name is all but obliterated. And best of all the rhododendron walk, giant trees whose red, pink, and purple blooms erupt into the spring skies like benign rockets.

Closer to the house are the two smaller gardens: the bestiary, a green zoo of fanciful creatures sculpted of ivy and boxwood; and the Irish garden, with its topiary harp, leprechauns perched on huge azalea toadstools, and a Red Hand of Ulster done in begonias.

The driver pulls up to the front portico, jumps out, and begins to extricate Sam's luggage. Sam quickly scoops up the square package from the front seat, and climbs out with it tucked under his briefcase and folded raincoat. He hurries past the driver and up the steps, where the bridegroom, his old pal Charlie, is waiting. Big hugs; bloody marvelous. The bride can't wait to meet him. And there's an unmarried sister. I've instructed her, says Charlie, to meet all your requirements. Because she's refused to marry Ludo.

Sam will have to make do with an attic room, sharing with Charlie's cousin, Sholto. They're squeezed, not having expected him till the last possible minute. Not to worry, though, and no apologies. Charlie assures him, When you said no, we considered calling off the wedding.

Sam is still carrying the box, shielded by his coat and briefcase, as they mount the third back stairway to the attic rooms. These were servants' quarters and the nursery for the Brit who built this pile, with his wife's money, in 1865.

Plus ça change, eh? says Sam, and Charlie obliges with a conspiratorial chuckle. We're here, he says.

Sam deposits his burdens on the bed that isn't covered with beautifully tailored tweeds. Any bulletins from the road warrior? he asks.

Charlie's laugh is affectionate, if slightly derisive. Ludo? Can't win, poor sod. But this rally's hardly serious. I mean it's Irish. I daresay he won't finish last, anyway. They're still hoping to make it here in time, barring the unforeseen.

In Ludo's case, says Sam, in a tone several shades darker than he intended, I wouldn't bar the unforeseen.

Charlie chooses to let this go. The loo, he says, is just on the left, two doors down. Throw on a sweater or something, we'll have a spin. In his honor. Unless you'd prefer tea with the bridesmaids? Two are rather nice.

A short ride, says Sam. Then a nap. Give me five minutes. Seven.

Right. Sorry, you're probably knackered. Jet lagging?

Not a bit. Against my religion.

See you in five, then. Seven.

Charlie shuts the door. Sam rips open the box, stares at the contents: a six-pack of diet Dr Pepper. There's a card: For Father McGurk. As per request: L.

Sam crumples the card, carefully slides the carton under his bed, slips on an Irish sweater, races down the stairs. Sean Harrison is at the bottom, feet planted apart, a boxer's stance. No how do you do. Did a package for me arrive with you? he says. We can't seem to find it.

Sam stammers, Yes sir. Afraid I've just opened it. By mistake. In my room.

Harrison's eyebrows go up. When exactly had you planned on delivering it to the addressee?

I'm afraid, Sam begins to improvise, I was actually planning to drink it all. Ludo knows I'm an addict. I allowed myself to think he sent it for me. Fact is he promised to. I'd said it was a condition for my coming. Kidding, of course.

A *quick* set of lies, anyway, Harrison says coldly. I'd like it delivered now, if you don't mind. Bring it to the library. There. He gestures with the point of his goatee, and turns his back.

Sam races up the stairs, retrieves the carton, and finds his way to the library. It could be the principal's office. He could be expelled. With a note to his mother.

Harrison is seated behind a desk that fills a bay window looking out over the Irish garden. His chair is turned around to face it. Come in, he says at Sam's knock. He doesn't turn the chair.

You do have a notion as to what might be in those cans, I assume, he says. And its value? Sam, isn't it?

Yes. I think I do, sir.

Then why would you attempt to shortstop it?

I don't know. Exactly.

I'll ask once more. Exactly.

I thought I might trade it for a part in the, uh, proceedings.

You thought that?

Well. Sam begins to mumble. I guess I wasn't, actually, thinking at all. I've had . . . some problems the last few days.

I know, Harrison says. Tell you what, Sam. We'll consider this incident closed for the moment. You'll interfere again at your considerable risk, though. And I'll hold Ludo equally liable for the slightest deviation, from any detail, of this weekend. Clear so far?

Yes. Sir.

There is a very slight pause. Then Harrison adds: I may have a role for you at that. I can promise you won't like it. But you have earned it. And I wouldn't mention this conversation. Not to Ludo. Or Charlie.

No. Sir.

Harrison abruptly swivels in his chair, drums his fingers lightly on the carton of root beer, then pulls one can free, tosses it to Sam. Drink up. *Slàinte!*

Sweating profusely in his heavy sweater, Sam gingerly peels back the tab, lifts the warm can with two shaking hands, closes his eyes, swallows.

Harrison's laugh explodes like an Irish thunderclap. What *did* you think it was?

The color has drained from Sam's face. He buckles and sinks into a chair.

Good lad, says Harrison, slapping his desk for emphasis. See you at dinner.

He is still chortling when Sam makes it to the door. Charlie is loitering just outside, wearing a curious expression. Not exactly chummy.

What? says Sam.

Nothing. I've never been invited in there alone. And you've never met him.

Based on this singular experience, Sam retorts, you're way ahead, pal. If you've never been called on that remarkable carpet, you're doing something right.

Well, marrying the daughter isn't it, let me tell you. My divorce doesn't help. Neither does being broke. Though I do send him my share of her rent every month; haven't missed once since I moved in. He never cashes the checks. Come on, we'll take the MG.

Maybe, says Sam, he likes it that you've got weird low-rent friends like me.

The Irish don't understand the concept of low-rent, my friend. They used to knock their roofs off to avoid paying any rent at all.

Funny, says Sam. I always thought it was you Brits who knocked their roofs off.

Whatever. Would you rather take the Lancia?

I think, Sam suddenly says, I need that nap.

The sun is out. Sudden, blinding. We are alone on a mountain road in Kerry, a veritable corniche, a white crease spiraling up the green slopes like a ski trail. Flanks of rounded hills rise and enfold us, like the thighs of some dangerous goddess we have dared to arouse.

With this light, the green turns so eerily bright that it hurts to look at it. As with a total eclipse, you must only glance sidelong, or backward through a keyhole. Knowing that if you are not a very careful witness to this miracle, you will surely never see another.

This green, this treacherous beauty, is what outcast poets write love songs about in the New World, forever mourning their loss. The ineffable color of an exile's grief. *"I'll Take You Home Again, Kathleen . . ."*

I know better than to suggest we stop for a minute to wonder at it. Ludo has his own way of celebrating. Turns up the music, sucks his finger, sips his Coke, puts on more speed.

I almost don't mind, so warmed am I, so embraced. Just to watch his jawline framed in pure emerald-studded light. Only later will I realize what song he happens to choose for this particular moment: *"Fifty Ways to Leave a Lover."*

Two of our fellow rally cars are at the curve just ahead; we close the distance, passing the Vitesse. The Sprite puts on another burst and vanishes as the road bends again.

Ludo guns it, and we're gaining. Even our music swells, pushing the golden air out of our way.

I imagine we are aflame, lit from within. Waves of fire dancing out of both sides. Playful, mischievous flames keeping time with the melody, improvising a magical ballet as they weave back up over the silver bonnet, reaching to catch each other's fingers, licking and rolling off the sparkling paint with liquid tongues. Look at that!

Ludo is already looking. We are in fact on fire. He pulls over gently onto the sliver of grassy verge between road and steep mountainside.

For an instant we are both transfixed, and I think it must feel like this, knowing one's child is trapped in a burning house. But is this burning car the house, or the child? At last I hear Ludo shouting, *Out!* I obey, mute and slow as in a dream. We stand together watching the fire dancers, ravenous now, consuming the molten silver tenderly, as though this were the climax of an ancient holy rite. Ludo's face is ashen, a classical mask of agony. The car is too hot for him to touch.

Minutes later another rally driver pulls up and stops. Tell the sweepers, Ludo whispers. The voice of a soldier guarding his fallen comrade. The other driver nods gravely, says nothing, climbs back in his car, thunders off.

I assume we are in mourning. Also that we are stranded.

He corrects me at once: I am stranded. He is going on, with the girls in the Reliant, which has just pulled up. They look stricken at the awful sight of us. He says, I'll find a tow truck; it needs to be flat-bedded. Don't move away from it. We'll send help as soon as we can.

He hesitates then, calculating fast. Making irrevocable decisions. Reaches in for his suitcase, box of music tapes, carry bag of champagne.

And he kisses me, tongue thrusting. Warm as the flames devouring his car.

I am not alone long. Avenger Tiger is just cresting the hill; I wave it down. Dangerous or not, I'm glad to see Mutch, and John Joe of the ice-blue gaze. I don't have to say a word. They're all over the car, assessing the damage. The flames are subsiding; it's almost cool enough to perform the autopsy. Mutch flicks the hood lever; the long sleek jaw opens slightly, like the mouth of a dental patient in mortal pain.

Is it really dead? I don't ask.

John Joe wraps his anorak over his hands, pries the hood open, props it up. Black smoke billows; the innards are still red-hot. He and Mutch peer inside. Melted white plastic covers everything, like boiled-over porridge.

Not fatal, Mutch decrees. Short somewhere, I'd say. Battery's gone. Want to squeeze in with us and go on? We can find someone to send back for it.

Better not, I decide. For several reasons. I can't even be sure if they're good ones.

Mutch seems to understand. Righti-o, he says cheerfully. I'm guessing you won't make it to Kyteler Manor, then.

His motor is roaring as he flings over his shoulder: Any message for Sam—if he's there?

They're gone before I can possibly respond, before I've even absorbed the meaning of what he's just told me.

By the time I understand, I am galvanized. Flagging down a farmer with a lorry load of doomed sheep. Riding twenty miles, trying not to echo their bleating cries of terror. The farmer takes me to a neighbor's shed, where I make a deal for a tow truck and flatbed trailer. Up into the mountains to search for the car, without signposts, landmarks, trail of bread crumbs.

The sun is long gone, replaced by soft, intimate rain, before we make it back to the shed. Another hour to find the short circuit, two more to fiddle with the wiring, locate a battery, improvise substitutes for exotic bits and bobs. This is a car whose like has surely never been met on a Kerry mountain road. Wiggle, wiggle.

The sky threatens further revenge for that dazzling morning as I set out to find Kyteler Manor on my own. Hoping I make it to the wedding. Before Ludo blows it up? Along with Sam? I force myself to repeat that, until it sinks in: Along with Sam.

At the bride's insistence, Charlie Baker's bachelor's dinner will not exclude women. When this was announced to Charlie's friends, it set off the usual rude jokes about hot-tempered redheads and how you couldn't say no to one you were about to marry, because of what she'd surely set fire to on her wedding night.

But Charlie had been living with Majella Harrison for more than a year. He had the battle scars to prove that she wasn't just a redhead. She was Sean Harrison's spoiled daughter, and she had twenty million pounds that said she could damn well have her way about anything. By now Charlie knew he'd always have the last word—as long as it was yes.

So he was willing to let his bride, her attendants, and a few others join the party. Majella's father could hardly refuse. But Sean did insist that the evening's program would not be changed. No concessions to feminine sensibilities.

Agreed, said Charlie.

Not, mind you, that they'd booked some hard-tit crumpet
to jump naked out of a cake and piss in a cup for fifty quid.
Every man here had surely seen enough of that.

Sean Harrison had more of an Irishman's tradition in
mind. Something not one of these sodding Brits and Yanks
would ever forget.

What he planned was just an old-fashioned sheep shagging. They'd go out to the tent he'd had put up deep in the
woods, beside the horse monument. After dinner. After
they'd all had a few jars, a wee brandy or two, some singing
and storytelling, speeches, the lot.

He'd use one of his own sheep. (Though not one of the
rare breeds.) And it wouldn't need to be killed. Necessarily.
They'd just queue up and have a go, one by one.

One of the lads would be assigned to make a video. Personal copies for the groom, best man, ushers, honored guests.

The crack, as they call a high old time in Ireland, would be
mighty.

And if the women couldn't handle it, they could sod off to
the sitting room and have a think about things. Females
need to be taught when to leave the men to it. Daughters no
less than wives.

As for the men, would any one of them dare refuse? And
let the others think what they surely would? Sean Harrison had no worries. Didn't he know that no man turns
down a command performance at Kyteler Manor? He
would go first, show them how it used to be done back in
Tuam. Then his close friends and associates would have a
go, men who'd been his mates since they were lads. Didn't

they grow up playing all the games together? Not just Gaelic football.

The rest of them would follow, surely. Like sheep.

Ludo's car, without Ludo, fits me like a natural shell. As if I were one of those tiny, perfect creatures who hold on for dear life to a reed blowing in an Irish sand dune. Pink, or pale yellow, with curving stripes like a sleek little hard candy. I'd seen them heaped, wet and sparkling, in a secret bone white crater called the Valley of Diamonds. They are the "diamonds." I am one now.

With Ludo gone, the controls leap to do my bidding almost before I issue the command. The gearshift, sensitive to my touch, responding like an eager lover. I'm strapped to a speeding bullet; I'm not driving—we've both been shot from a cannon. Never so fast. Never so sure. There's pure adrenaline in the fuel tank. We may look a mess, me with my streaming hair and the fear in my eyes, the car with all the beautiful silver skin peeled off its nose. But we don't care; we are flying together like champion dancing partners, whirling dervishes. Up on two wheels as we turn, tipsy and light, never making a sound till we touch down, screaming. The secrecy of our affair makes us giggle. Passion makes us bold. Yes, I whisper to it, croon to it. Tighter, tighter. Yes!

We came to a sudden ninety-degree turn; I didn't brake in time, or perhaps at all. The road was shining, possibly wet. Someone was coming for us too fast through the hedgerow. We slid or danced gracefully off the road and came to a stop, nuzzling a telegraph pole. It was the only obstacle to a sheer drop down the mountain.

A hail of forgotten stones and seashells, long hidden under the passenger seat, now rose in protest, mysteriously, silently, to hurl themselves at the windshield, etching an exquisite cobweb in the glass. I watched their flight, marveling at their sudden, furious life force, their suicidal leap, the delicacy of their destructive art.

I had at first no sensation of actually striking the pole. When I realized it, I said aloud, We're not dead. And it's not raining. I was laughing when the blue minivan drew up alongside us, and the priest jumped out.

He was very calm, operating like a surgeon in a battlefield. The engine was still running; only the front bumper embraced the pole, putting our nose out of joint. Father McGurk whistled softly as he worked to free us, with the astonishing array of tools that lived in his van. After a while, he inquired politely: Was I a tourist? American? I told him I was a writer, which caused him to smile. He was, he explained, a reader. Chiefly of one book, which he was currently reading for the eleventh time. It was a historical work, about the sinking of the *Titanic*, that great unsinkable ocean liner whose maiden voyage was its last. In 1912 the *Titanic* struck an iceberg and went down in the North Sea; for Father McGurk it remained the century's most potent symbol of pride going before a fall. British pride, of course. Which to this Irish priest was no coincidence. Nor was the fact that many of the fifteen hundred souls lost in the icy waters were desperate Irishmen escaping to a New World.

Laboring now over Ludo's pride and joy, the priest went on about that great ship, telling the tale like a parable from the Gospel. Arrogant Brits scrambling over their handful of lifeboats, still wearing their evening clothes. Irish peasants locked below in steerage as the icy waters rose to claim them. No one told them there weren't enough lifeboats; that there was no place in any boat for them.

When at last a few of them rose up and broke down doors, they found themselves in a vast, splendid, empty dining room. Lamps still glowing on the abandoned tables. Silver trolleys rolling like loose cannons across the gleaming ballroom floor.

And the shining eyes of an Irish lass, about to drown in the frozen sea, whose last vision this was. She cries, ecstatic as any martyred saint: *First class*!

The priest stood up; we were free. We stood in the rain and shook hands. He asked if I knew my way from here, and I told him where I was going. He said as it happened he was going that way too.

I watched him hang his tools in the back of the van, fitting each one precisely into the place on the wall where its outline was drawn.

It occurred to me that Father McGurk believed, as devoutly as those he hated, in the divine order of his universe. Arrogant Brits scrambling for lifeboats. Irish going under.

And did I know, he asked, the name of the fellow who wrote that story of the *Titanic*? I did, but I let him tell me. Lord, he said. The message was apocalyptic.

What I didn't know was what else he carried in the back of his van.

The bachelor's dinner was going well. The joint—lamb, as it happened—pink-centered and perfectly cooked. Every English schoolboy's favorite pudding: treacle tart. Rivers of Irish whiskey, excellent wine, Guinness, brandy, and cigars. They had pipers in kilts piping from the turrets, lit by floodlights and a full moon.

They sang chorus after chorus of "Waltzing Matilda," and traded uproarious secrets of Charlie Baker's misspent youth.

Then it was time for the sheep shagging. They trooped, singing, into the woods, carrying torches. Sam whispered to Charlie, Remember the bestiality scene in that film *Everything You Always Wanted to Know About Sex*?

Charlie's chuckle seems somewhat strained. Woody Allen's worst movie ever, he says. The sheep was brilliant, though.

Remember, Sam persists, how the psychiatrist sends the sheep flowers? Books the bridal suite in a fancy hotel? And she still won't put out?

Gentlemen! Sean Harrison's voice booms from the tent's hidden loudspeakers. You're all very welcome! We're here with a lovely creature called Ginger. Because tonight, every man here is Fred!

Self-conscious, then hearty, laughter as two men lead the sheep into the tent, down an aisle, up onto a platform trimmed with white flowers. She is white-faced, massive, heavy-fleeced. Cameras begin to flash, front, back, both sides. The sheep's pale eyes blink in the lights. There's a band playing, keeping the mood lively. Stockbrokers and lawyers, business leaders and career diplomats grow subdued as they jostle into a ragged queue, avoiding eye contact.

There's a brief pause. Sean turns abruptly, mounts the platform, addresses Ginger's broad back. He moves; the sheep bleats a futile protest, which sets off a shock wave of frenzied whooping and laughter. The music is suddenly louder, faster, whipping the excitement into a froth. It's a circus band's accompaniment for the crowd's favorite clown act: miming a striptease in baggy pants.

Sean, grinning, straightens up, steps aside quickly, beckons to his new English son-in-law. Charlie will have a bloody great fortune tomorrow for his indignity tonight. He does what he's bid, as he will from now on.

Man after man steps forward, performs to lusty cheers, steps down. Stockbrokers and lawyers, Irishmen and Brits. Sheep shaggers all.

Sam keeps edging back to the end of the line. He is eyeing the rear flap of the tent when Sean fixes him with a steely look, an almost imperceptible shake of the head: Don't even think about it.

Most of the women have declined the invitation to watch the fun. Only the stubborn bride and two stalwart friends have stayed, cringing in their pretty dresses against the canvas walls, forcing bold smiles when anyone looks their way.

Majella's glazed eyes were seen to close only once, at the instant Charlie ejaculated.

Ginger will have to be slaughtered tomorrow, after all. Sean is glad he didn't use one of the Carriedales.

Walking back through the woods, Sean finds Sam. There now, he says. Not so bad at all, was it?

No sir, Sam says carefully. I got—into it.

Good lad. Knew you would. Half a million Irishmen can't be wrong. He slips a heavy, comradely arm around Sam's shoulder. Join me in the library after a bit. Half an hour, say. We'll go over the plan for tomorrow. That role I had in mind for you. If you still want it.

Sam hesitates. Sir, is all he says.

Half an hour later, they face each other across the gleaming mahogany field that is Harrison's library desk. This time Sean's chair is facing front. There is nothing on the desk but a silver tray, with two heavy crystal tumblers and a decanter of the best.

I've meant to say, Sean begins, how deeply I regret what happened to you in New York. It was never part of any plan, believe me. I'd have stopped it if I'd been told.

I haven't been told much myself, sir, says Sam. Only that Ludo had some deal going, with some . . . people we both know. If I helped, he said, it would be worth some money. Enough to pay off serious bills. And my—Mary Jo—

Your mother, yes. Sean's smile is a shade condescending. I recall Ludo saying she might be persuaded to deliver a parcel for us. Sensitive material—

Not Dr Pepper.

Bits and pieces he had to bring over in his car.

Explosives?

Not as such.

Where are they now? Where's Ludo? And my—and the car. And the sensitive material.

Ah, says Sean. They've had a bit of a breakdown. Nobody hurt. He'll be here tomorrow, I'm sending a helicopter for him. I gather the car, and your mother, are waiting for repairs.

And the materials?

I'd say Ludo will have them.

What's my role?

Just to make that delivery. To a fellow Yank. You'll meet tomorrow. We've been working on the deal. Should have it all settled before the reception.

And if not?

We have a contingency plan. Needn't concern you for the moment.

Why isn't Ludo delivering it himself?

Ludo negotiates. He no longer delivers.

You're not going to tell me what I'm handling.

Sure, why wouldn't I? Sean spreads his hands, nothing up the sleeves. It's only a thing you Yanks have plenty of, but you worry about other people having some too. "The wrong hands," is how you like to put it. And believe me, I understand.

Are there any, Sam says slowly, "wrong hands" invited to the wedding?

Ah, now, how would I know? Wrong is such a changeable notion. In my business, I find it useful only to describe people who can't pay what they owe.

Why trust me, then?

I don't trust you a bit. You're bold, though. Stealing from me, right under my nose. I caught you; that should make you careful when you're working for me. And you are.

I don't—

Sean opens a drawer, pulls out a folder. Your bills have been paid. Ludo's sent the receipts here. Quite considerable. And your ticket and this check—tomorrow's payment. COD. He holds up the check.

Sam swallows. Could I die from carrying this—parcel? Could I die if I refuse? And my—mother too?

Oh, yes. Yes to all those questions. Especially if you fuck up.

There is a silence. Sean glances at his watch.

Mr. Harrison. Whose side are you on?

Side? Sean frowns, as if he's never encountered the word. I'm an entrepreneur. Like Ludo. And not unlike you. Shag or be shagged, my boy. By the way, know what a ha-ha is?

Ha-ha?

It's a deep trench. If you have sheep, you dig it out in the field. Line it with rocks, very elaborate. You don't want a fence; spoils your view. This is invisible from the house, d'you see. And the sheep can't see it either. But if they try to make a move, get too close, you can guess what happens. Don't forget the name: ha-ha. I believe the Brits invented it.

He looks again at his watch. Get some sleep, Sam. You're shagged out.

For Victoria Anne, tomorrow creeps in its petty pace, even when her own tires shriek to the contrary. Don't lift, *don't lift*, she scolds her foot, as though it could serve as a royal whipping boy. *Now, full gas!* She has a passion for hitting top speed in the turns, braking only in panic.

So it was no surprise that "Zan Playfair," finishing the 1,500-mile rally in a respectable third place, was still in too much of a hurry to stay for the prize giving, the closing night party, the photo finish.

Giles, the brilliant co-driver whose head never lifted from the map on his knees, was disappointed. But Zan would never let him forget whose idea it was to take a shortcut over a sea cliff, which almost certainly cost them the trophy.

In any case there were a hundred details that had to be looked after at home. Not that others weren't looking after them. But for Victoria Anne, flying on automatic means never letting go of the controls anyway.

The entire London phase of the operation had been locked into place a week ago, before her flight to Belfast for the start of the rally. This time tomorrow there is to be a transatlantic satellite signal. A phone call, U.S.A. direct: targets at both ends of the wire erupting at once. U.K. and U.S.A. coming together, bursting apart. A special relationship. Big Ben strikes the hour, on the fourth note, da dum, di *dum*: both houses of Parliament, gone. The guard changes at Buckingham Palace; Christopher Robin goes down with Alice. The Queen is in the parlor, eating bread and honey. Finally, she is what she eats.

So it would go in New York; the UN, Saks Fifth Avenue, golden Prometheus watching the skaters at Rockefeller Center. In Washington, Lincoln topples off his white marble chair. Unknown soldier rises from his tomb, rekindled in his own eternal flame. Ashes to ashes.

Vicky had ordered a pinch of powder reserved for a personal target. Sentimental, perhaps. But she wanted it. Just sprinkled in the Thames from Waterloo Bridge, where the young dancer in the old film flung her dishonored body, choosing death over love. She had sold herself, so she wasn't entitled to life either. To Vicky, contaminating the river seemed sweet savage justice. This rebel princess always saw herself as that star-crossed dancer. Life without love or honor. A royal pain.

But that is all tomorrow. Right now, Vicky is only a passenger in a car, innocent of the bloody history that already lies under her wheels on this Irish road. Giles is driving; odd to see his soft, round face raised up from his maps, the pale eyes gazing anxiously at what lies ahead. He's dropping her off at Dublin airport. It will take him all day for the ferry and the drive across; leaving the car with her mechanic in Cheltenham; catching a train back to London. By then everything should be over, bar the shouting. It's unlikely she'll ever see him again.

Good-bye, dear boy, Giles sighs. Zan tosses his bright hair, in that endearing pony gesture. As the glass door closes between them, Giles is smoothing the Lotus's creamy tonneau cover into place. It's a lover's gesture. Snap, snap.

He should have said no. It wasn't even simple greed. If only he could curb his irrepressible prankster's urge to yank the cloth out from under the feast. Expertly, of course. No spills, no shattering of glass. When Ludo breaks up a party, you scarcely remember what it was like before. Now he surveys this trendy pub in disgust. Dublin arts yuppies, gold hoops and studs winking from every orifice. Trophies over the bar: photos of small men holding up big fish; rotted boots dangling on fishing lines; rusted Texas license plates; poems protesting a gold rush on a holy mountain. Christ. Why hadn't he just hung up? Of all the cretins to do an unexpected bit of business with. And the bastard hasn't shown up. They all run on Irish time, even when they're blowing up the civilized world.

On the other hand, he might as well argue with himself. A quick, silent, painless deal. Wire transfer of the money. No fingerprints on the merchandise. Damn certain of that. Vicky would cut him dead. Harrison would make sure he was.

All they needed was a handful of dust. Enough to take care of some bad guy who had proved a disappointment to his associates. There had been a rash of these in the last year. Russian businessmen just getting sick and then dying horribly. You'd have to know the nature of their business to figure out why they all happened to die in this particular agonizing way, one after another. Just when their export business was beginning to pick up.

Ludo could tell you it was all right to wonder about this, but not too safe to have all the answers, not even from a careful distance. You've got a beautiful profile, you keep it very low indeed.

But someone had tipped Mutch that Ludo was approachable. A one-off deal or, all going well, the first of several. One had heard that competition was beginning to heat up in a number of new markets. Ludo's Yale economics professor had hammered home the old lesson: supply and demand, two blades of a scissors. In black marketing, however, Ludo found that one blade was often sharper and, furthermore, a screw was sometimes missing at the hinge. Without the screw, the scissors had no snicker-snack.

Being the screw, the one on whom things hinged, was not unappealing. Being the agent for snicker-snack was positively brilliant.

Mutch has arrived. Ludo barely nods: Let's get to it.

You have it.

Of course.

Wire transfer to your New York account? London?

Zurich.

Fine, says Mutch. Once we've established that you're delivering what we need.

Ludo shakes his head. I haven't got time. Helicopter's collecting me—

We have a lab set up, says Mutch smoothly. Go have

breakfast at the Shelburne. Their scones are good. I imagine you do like fucking scones.

Ludo scowls at his watch.

Mutch pats his pocket.

I don't, says Ludo, actually know whose right-hand man you are.

Mutch grins, draws his right hand out, displays the two missing fingers. Ah, sure you do, he says.

Ludo hesitates.

The Shelburne, then? My people salute your people. He holds up a rude middle finger.

Ludo rolls his eyes, hands over a small metal box. Mutch pockets it quickly.

They leave separately, Mutch stopping in the Gents on the way out. Ludo, tunneling through smoke and the sweet stench of Guinness, leather, and sweat, doesn't notice the girl sitting alone in the snug closest to the street door. At a glance you'd say she wasn't out of place. Skimpy black clothes, heavy boots, stark makeup, a certain haunted look around the black-rimmed eyes.

She isn't Irish, though. She's been here only a few days. Just long enough to have learned the mysterious facts of life in this strange country: nothing you do is unseen. Nowhere you go is a private place.

And she has certainly seen Ludo; she's been watching him the entire time he's been here.

She was also astonished to see, and to recognize, the man

who joined him. She had glimpsed this person only once, across a courtyard, grappling with a bag on a rain-slick stair. He dropped it and ran, vaulting over a high stone wall. There was fire behind him; in the light she saw him raise a hand to his face. Right hand with missing fingers. Just before something blew up, and a gun fired, and she was left for dead.

Father McGurk has stopped to call at his sister's. The one who is still a nun, and still on speaking terms with him. The other sister left the religious life fifteen years ago, pleading a slight heart condition. It never seemed to flare up again.

Since then Agnes, the religious dropout, has indulged all her consuming passions: envy, avarice, gaudy clothes, and spiteful gossip. She has a sharp eye and a keen little nose for the kind of detail that can get others into terrible trouble, while you sit quite still. A small talent, well nourished and honed by convent life, it has since matured into something very like genius.

Agnes is nearly sixty now, but there has been no letup in the quarreling between her and her brother over property left by their late father, including the lucrative pub license. Even less muted is her righteous anger over the scandal that drove Father McGurk from his parish, and eventually from Ireland. Altar boys. The family never mentions it.

Sheila, the younger sister who is still a nun, and who keeps in contact with Father McGurk, lives the quiet convent life in Monkstown, a seaside Dublin suburb. Times are hard; for years, the order has made ends meet by renting a few rooms to tourists and running a small souvenir shop on the convent grounds. Tea towels with shamrocks; Aran sweaters; tweed caps. The caps are made by the handicapped in a Tipperary factory. They are especially popular with Frenchmen on bus tours. That is to say, the Frenchmen try on every cap in the shop, admire themselves in all the mirrors, rarely buy anything. When the bus driver sounds the horn for departure, the Frenchmen leave their blizzard of rejected caps scattered over the counters, and the nuns, who still wear veils, rush about tidying up, gauzy black panels fluttering around them like insect wings.

The guest rooms are simple and austere, bordering on monastic. The sisters have made few concessions to transient commerce. TV sets, yes, but discreetly hidden behind cabinet doors that may be unlocked on request. Crucifix over each bed. Pictures of Jesus, with lurid bleeding heart and reproachful, pursuing eyes, still monitor the hall stairway.

Breakfast is served up with a radio program of non-stop hymns. Even the weather report sounds like a sermon, dropping as the gentle rain upon the individual boxes of high-fiber cereal beneath.

On Father McGurk's rare visits home, he'll stay the night in the convent guest house; let his sister Sheila rabbit on about old times, the neighbors, and relations. Once in a while she'll ring them up, announce his visit as if it's grand news, beg them to drop by for a cuppa. Most of them are usually busy, sorry to miss old Des. Agnes always is. Busy, not sorry.

This time, however, Sheila senses something seriously

wrong with her brother. Something new. He's a born fidgeter, is Des, but today his unease is of another order. He keeps writing furtive notes to himself, hiding them in that book he's always reading. Won't sit still a minute. Now he's off for a walk along the strand. Alone.

She watches his gaunt figure from the shop window. When it disappears she says a quick prayer, and rings up Agnes. Is there some new trouble between them? No? Well then, would Agnes ever drop by and say a loving word? Agnes says she'll have a think about it.

Leaving the blue van locked in the convent's car park, Father McGurk sets off across the terrace road and down a flight of steps to the narrow strip of sand. He inhales deeply, gratefully, and begins to stride with long purposeful steps, head bowed against the punishing wind.

There's a solitary boy collecting mussels down at the far curve of the bay. Father McGurk stands watching the waves lap over the lad's green boots, then moves slowly toward him.

The boy turns, touches his cap. Good day, Father.

Lovely and fresh, isn't it? The boy nods, turning back to his task. Prying the stubborn shells from the rocks, piling the slow harvest into his plastic sack. The waves rise higher, covering his boots to the rim. His thin fingers are quite raw from the struggle.

For Father McGurk, the boy shimmers in the light like an image from the Great Famine. Women wading out from shore to gather the limpets that clung to rocks in the sea. Limpets to boil for a thin broth. But the sea was fierce, and the women's boots filled with it, even as their heavy clothes weighed them down. The work was slow and dangerous, the yield pitifully small. And so their men pleaded with the bishops: Let the women go into the sea without those heavy clothes. Free of the thick layers of skirts and flannel, they could wade out beyond the treacherous current and gather enough food to keep their families alive.

For modesty, for tradition, for fear of the Lord's wrath, the bishops refused. The women kept on with their work as before; their boots filled; their sodden clothes tangled relentlessly around their bodies like winding sheets. And they were swept away. Enrobed in their modesty for the sea to claim them.

Father McGurk, an epiphany of love rising in him, moves still closer to the boy, rehearsing what to say before he will permit himself to touch him.

While her brother dallies at the shore, Agnes arrives at the convent guest house, noting the blue van in the car park. Almost without a thought, she tries the doors.

It is no secret, however, that the guest rooms have no locks on their doors. And so it happens that when a German tour bus pulls up to the shop, Sheila bustles off, and Agnes finds her way to her brother's door. It isn't difficult; only three guest rooms, only one occupied. The key to the van is right there on the dresser, with Des's favorite book, *A Night to Re-*

member, which is, she observes with disapproval, better thumbed than the Bible beside it.

Bits of torn scrap paper protrude from the book like page markers. She pulls out one or two. Mystifying notes, scientific symbols. Diagrams, seemingly of mechanical devices. Wires and directions for connecting them. She can't make sense of anything, but she has a neighbor who fixes clocks and broken toasters. So she pockets a couple of the drawings. That Des. She shakes her head. A tinker.

Then, with the van key in her hand, she marches out to the car park. Within seconds, she's rummaging with the considerable skills of a veteran convent school snoop, behind the curtain of her brother's inner sanctum. There, tucked behind an odd-shaped metal box, is a manual about explosives. Agnes freezes for a fraction of a second. Then she moves like Irish lightning. Drums labeled with Cyrillic characters. A suitcase with checked baggage stubs from a German airline. What should she take? Quick—one of those. The drum with Russian letters is heavy as lead; she'll manage. She moves the others closer together, climbs out of the van, locks up, and runs to her own car. It will just about fit in the boot; there's an old blanket. . . . As if it were a dead body. Her famous dicky heart thrashes like a wild thing in its cage. She wills herself to calm down, to walk slowly, to find her sister in the souvenir shop. Nothing has happened, she tells herself in her sternest mother superior voice.

Sheila stares at her sister's scarlet, sweating face. Mother of God, what is it? she cries, crossing herself. Your heart—

Agnes shrieks, Where is Des going when he leaves you?

Sure don't I know where, says Sheila proudly. It's to the Harrison wedding down at Kyteler Manor. The daughter's marrying a Brit, so she is. Yet they've asked Des—Sean Harrison himself asked our Des—to perform a proper Catholic ceremony in the woods.

Agnes is trying hard not to give herself away. It's no use. She gasps, crosses herself. May God help us, Sheila! You're not serious.

Indeed I am, says Sheila, indignant now and defensive too. Didn't he give me the wedding program himself? I've it here, look. With his name engraved in gold. Now!

She flounces off, back to her post at the cash register.

Agnes stares at the elegant little booklet with its golden tassel, its delicate pen-and-ink portrait of the old manor house. When her hands begin to tremble, she flings the program from her as though it had a power, and makes another furtive sign of the cross.

But with it something alters; her expression softens from fear to a kind of awe. This was some miracle, surely. Like tears of blood on a holy statue. Resolute, she retrieves the precious booklet, runs her finger over the shining raised letters of her brother's name. Testing them. That surge of power she felt a moment ago seemed as real. Must be real. Must be hers. Is hers.

If she moves with great care this day, there will be an end to all trouble with her brother. That brother who will be punished at last. God's will. Agnes only His handmaid.

House, land, pub license, will fall then, like windfall apples, to her innocent waiting hand. Agnes McGurk. Woman of God. Woman of property. She crosses herself one last time. A quick bend of the knee for good measure.

Foolish Sheila is still tending her flock of tourists in unruly Aran sweaters, when her sister appears at the window, frantically signaling good-bye. Pointing elaborately at the little watch pinned to her peacock blue lapel.

Wait, Sheila calls softly, abandoning a customer with a nice long shipping list for America. By the time she reaches the door, Agnes's car engine is running.

Sheila sighs. Such a difficult family. She must try harder for Des's next visit. Where can he have walked to? Clarke's pub, would be her guess. She sighs again.

Agnes, speeding homeward, weighs her interesting options. Call the local *garda* station. That Captain Nelligan knows her alarms never prove false. Indeed, on the rare occasion Agnes McGurk is not an actual eyewitness to a misdeed, it's assumed she'll have a full report within minutes, from her vast network of spies. She could tell the *gardai* what is said when any two persons of opposite sexes chance to meet on a street corner. Or what Timmy Gallagher of Monkstown ordered for dinner with a certain widow in a certain hotel one hundred miles away in Cork City.

Any husband who goes missing after a domestic spat will be found within an hour, at most two, of the moment Agnes McGurk is notified. Based on what she knows already, or has good reason to suspect, the *gardai* will find that man's car parked exactly where it shouldn't be. Anywhere in Ireland.

So if she calls on Captain Nelligan, the young man at the front desk will say, Yes, ma'am, and summon the captain at once. He will know how important it must be for her to make a personal call. Terrorists, she will whisper to Nelligan. Bombs. Sean Harrison. Yes, ma'am!

This is certainly gratifying. But perhaps not altogether wise. In the long run, better an anonymous call to the captain of a *garda* station nearer to Kyteler Manor itself. No one need know the caller's identity. Anonymous tip. She reads this all the time in the paper. Based on an anonymous tip, police were able to track down . . .

Better so. Better a moment of self-sacrifice, a glory declined, than another blow to the family. And this blow mortal. Not even Agnes could hold up her head as Judas the betrayer. On the other hand . . .

E I G H T

Enjoy Ocasio is on the road again. Slumped and half-conscious between two grim-faced men in an unmarked gray sedan with British plates. They're heading west out of Dublin, in the same tense silence they've kept since Dublin released her to their custody, three hours ago.

Suddenly she straightens up. Wide awake. Ludo's car! She points at a battered silver sports car nosing out of a hidden side road just ahead of them.

You sure? says the driver. It's had some beating. Woman driver. Nobody else. Going pretty fast, too.

Enjoy shrugs. Maybe not. But there's a sticker on its side, with a number: 63.

Rally number, says the man who isn't driving. The sedan puts on speed as they pull closer, then pass the silver car. Enjoy says, I know. It's Sam's mother. She was with him. Sam said—

Who is Sam? says the driver. He doesn't trust this little

punk for a minute. Dublin picked her up in a hospital down in Mayo. Locals found her alive when they cleaned up after the raid on that lodge. She had a new gunshot wound and an old jagged cut that wasn't healing. The only other thing the locals found was a pickle jar full of weapons-grade plutonium. She didn't know squat about that. Didn't know where she was or how she got there. Priest in a blue van, she said. And meeting some character called Ludo at a society wedding. She didn't look like any society's invited guest. Didn't even know where the wedding was.

María Luz Encarnita Ocasio y Figueroa. No record, no apparent link to any paramilitary organization. A decoy, London's best guess. Somebody put her in that van, left her and the pickle jar for the locals to find.

While something big was going on someplace else. Their orders are to keep her till she leads them to it. Or to the character called Ludo.

So who is Sam? They want to know.

They were going to hurt him, Enjoy says. They tied him up, then they tied me too. I think Ludo told them to do it. It was Ludo I saw in the pub, before. I *told* you. With the other. The one with missing fingers. You didn't understand.

They nod. They understand now.

Think he'll be glad to see you? says the driver. Sam?

She says, He brought me here. To help or to hurt me I don't know.

What if, says the man who isn't driving, what if it wasn't to help *or* hurt you? Just to use you for bait?

What is bait? Enjoy asks.

The man smiles. You put a little shrimp or worm on a hook. To go fishing. He casts an imaginary fly.

Enjoy frowns. What fish?

Us, says the driver, pulling to a stop well beyond the woman in the silver car. Let's get you into that vehicle.

Kyteler Manor is not yet awake for the serious business of this day. For caterers and house staff to begin sidestepping each other, smiling warily. Who will be blamed later for the broken glass, the roses that droop, the cigarette burn on the library sofa? Weekend guests have not yet rung for their coffee; photographers have not begun to snake coils of cable through the topiary garden.

But Chitra Harrison is puttering in the kitchen. Feeding the four wolfhounds, which requires cooking her special chicken and lamb in the tandoor. Polishing her prize collection of miniature crystal figurines. She won't let staff touch her angels and unicorns, her mice and men. They're fragile, but that isn't why. She likes the excuse to touch them, to rub them, then to stand in rapturous gaze at the sight of them, in their dazzling world of mirrored lakes and mountains, every facet dancing in a hundred slices of cold, perfectly pure white light. But in the pre-dawn chill of this festive day, even these refuse to console her.

The telephone call came at two o'clock. Sean answered, and spent twenty minutes pleading with the caller. Abject pleading, in a lover's desperate voice that Chitra has never heard.

Who was that?

Business, he said. Problems.

Who? she persisted.

Vicky, actually. Business.

You said that. What did she say that made you beg like that? You never beg.

I had to apologize. What she wants won't be happening when she wants it. Logistics. We can't afford to mess up what's going on right here today. She never takes no.

Chitra hesitates, weighing all this with care. No, she says then. You're involved with her. I've known it. I just haven't said it. You just never let it into my bed.

With that she gets up. Her heavy body still gleams with the perfumed oil she rubs on, in all her folds and creases, at bedtime, for his nightly pleasure. Last night, however, following the bachelor's party, the bedside *Kama Sutra*, lavishly illustrated, remained untouched, as did she.

Then came the telephone call.

Ah, Chit, Sean begins, please don't start this today. He watches with regret as she folds away her heavy golden breasts, covers the swell of her belly and soft thighs. These are his things.

She pauses before buttoning. Tell me you wouldn't rather fuck a princess than a dirty wog.

Chit! Who's the dirty Mick you married, then? Come back to bed. Take those clothes off. I want my things.

My family, she says without moving, thought my marrying you would be good for business. Only my mother warned me.

Chit, please!

167

And you're still fucking her.

Who?

Princess who.

She finishes encasing her body in some voluminous red garment. He sighs. Without clothes, oiled and fragrant, she is a luscious exotic fruit. Sheela-na-gig, fertility symbol swollen with forbidden juice. Dressed, she is rather a plump wog. Though he does quite like to see her teeter on stiletto heels.

When she slams the door, he rolls over to seek refuge in a couple of hours' sleep.

After that, she was busier than usual in the kitchen. Besides the wolfhounds' curry and the crystal miniatures, there was something she needed to do for Sean.

Charlie Baker, nervous bridegroom, hasn't slept much either. Feeling definitely queasy, he'd have to say, since ejaculating into that sheep's arse. Christ, these people. For the first time in the two years since his discovery that Majella Harrison's small but perky tits tasted of real money, he isn't a hundred percent sure he's doing the right thing.

With the first streaks of gray watery light in the sky, he's up and pounding on Sam's door. We need to drive, he shouts. Now. Charlie's obnoxious cousin Sholto answers with a stream of groggy expletives, but finally kicks Sam, who eventually staggers to the door.

Drive, now? he mutters.

Come on, we'll take Sean's favorite Jag, the yellow one.

We can do the Achill coast drive, it's brilliant. Only road in Ireland where I've ever seen a sign that says Test Your Brakes.

Achill? Sam is still barely awake. It's way the hell on the other coast.

Two and a half hours, tops. You can drive. Nobody will be looking for us before two o'clock. Come on, maybe we'll run into Ludo. Race him back.

His car broke down, remember? He's coming by helicopter.

Oh, right. So he'll be here to see us coming. In a *really* fast car. Come *on*.

Sam is half dressed before he remembers what he's got to do today, before the wedding. A certain delivery. Megadeath in a tin box. Christ. He finishes dressing and bounds down the back stairs. Charlie is outside in the morning mist, leaning against a golden teardrop diamond of a car. He's got on an ancient leather motoring coat that matches exactly. And goggles. Looks like a twenties cigarette poster. Sam sighs.

Charlie, I can't go. I promised to do something for—your, uh, father-in-law.

Fuck him, says Charlie cheerfully. After five o'clock today, we'll take his orders forever. Like we did last night. Get in.

Sam gets in.

Seated at a window table in Dublin's most elegant hotel lobby, Ludo is in a rare celebratory mood. Scarcely a twinge about not winning the rally.

The pea-size sample he gave Mutch to test has met all requirements; he's handed over his special box of music tapes. High-quality stuff. Worth plenty to the discerning collector. Plenty has in fact already been wire transferred to Ludo's private Swiss corporate account. One of them. And the sun isn't even up. Early days in the life of this apocalypse.

He's packed and ready, it's half an hour to the heliport, time for kippers and a scone. Time to entertain a jumble of passing thoughts: Sam's mother, Vicky, Sean Harrison, finding a decent silver spray paint for the Alfa. Not disturbing thoughts, actually, not any of them.

For Ludo, in fact, the dawn of this day seems nothing short of brilliant. By the end of it, nothing may be the same. On the other hand nothing much may happen. A few quid changing hands one way or another. Cargo moving, decimal points shifting on distant computer screens. Targets blown. Or not. Blips that pass in the night.

The scone is delicious. He lights a cigarette. No one comes to point out the No Smoking sign on his table.

N I N E

~⌣~

How could I not stop and pick up that girl? Standing in the rain, shivering, with her thumb out, her bandaged arm getting soaked. Looking like a New York street kid abandoned by her pimp.

By the time my conscience wins out over my shattered nerves, she has to run the length of two city blocks to where I've stopped. She makes it.

Thanks, she gasps, shaking herself like a spaniel, spattering me, the seats, the windshield.

Oh, sorry. What happened to your car?

Shit, I say, wiping the glass with my bare hand. As in Shit happens.

She giggles appreciatively. You're Sam's mother. I knew it.

I freeze. Who are you?

Enjoy Ocasio.

I know the name. Who could forget the name?

She says, He's here, you know. Sam.

I know. Why are you? Here.

Haven't a clue. She says this wearily, like someone who's had to repeat it too many times. Sam told me to come. He set it up. Something to do with Ludo. Where is Ludo anyway?

Since I can't answer that, I say, Doesn't everything have something to do with Ludo? Where are you going? Do you know that, at least?

She's busy with her hair, trying to dry it with her good hand. It isn't working.

I repeat the question. Where to?

She shrugs. Wherever you're going is fine.

Enjoy, I say carefully. Do you have a hunch about what's going on?

Do you?

This is evasive. I'm beginning to feel a prickly sensation at the back of my neck. Like when I first thought Ludo had a bomb in the car.

Sam is in trouble, I say. In case she cares. But this elicits rude laughter. Yeah, right, she says. Look at me. Bullet here. Slashed there. One way and another, Sam got me these.

All of a sudden I don't want to know what she might want to tell me. Also I notice a gray sedan in my rearview mirror. It's been there some time. Friends of yours?

No, she says. Cops. They want Ludo.

With something of a shock, I realize that as of this moment I don't. I try saying it aloud: I. Don't. Want. Ludo. It's exhilarating. I breathe deeply. Possibly I'm about to grow up. Hang on, I tell Enjoy Ocasio.

TEN

Last time I stopped for gas, I got directions. We're maybe five miles from Kyteler Manor. Three T-junctions, right, left, right. Old church opposite new church. Stone bridge . . .

Suddenly there's a helicopter overhead. A blue van directly in front of me, and a yellow Jag coming the other way. Very fast.

Enjoy screams. That van! It's the priest! The fire, the explosion! It's him, *mira*! Look, that red curtain blowing—

She makes no sense at all. Yet somehow I know I have to stop that van. We're coming to one of those impossible right-angle turns. The stone bridge, diagonal yellow-and-black warning stripes, white diamond sign with the black spot signifying Death, Here. No brakes. Full gas. Now.

We're gaining on him. He speeds up. Why is that Jag coming so fast—

Enjoy screams again as she rolls to the floor, curls up in a ball wedged under the dash. She never buckled up. I let go of the wheel then and hurl myself across both seats. Backward. Feet shoved flat against one door, head, buried in my arms, slammed against the other. As if my whole body wants to burst the car open at the sides. Inside my tightly shut eyes is a huge black spot, spreading. Death, Here.

It dawned on me later—oh, much later—that Ludo's car died saving us. If we'd been in a nice new Japanese plastic box, like the blue van, we would have covered the stone wall with new stripes, all red. The van folded up in pleats before the fire melted it down. The driver, Rev. Des McGurk, apparently died instantly.

The yellow Jag was totaled too. Charlie Baker, the reluctant bridegroom, went through his father-in-law's windshield. He survived, but both legs were broken, along with his engagement to Majella Harrison.

Sam, who was driving, got away with fractured ribs, internal injuries, and a slight concussion. Enjoy Ocasio must have forgiven him; she slept in a cot next to his hospital bed until he was out of danger. That Ulster's Red Hand of hers flung across his body. Someone finally told her the reference. Two giants raced their boats across the Irish Sea. First to touch the land of Ulster would claim it. The boats were coming in to shore, their bows still level; one giant cut off his own hand and flung it onto the land. Ulster was his.

The police found several sealed canisters and drums of radioactive material strewn over the road. Had any of it exploded in the collision, it would have wiped out most of Counties Kildare, Meath, and Westmeath. Ireland's green heart. Arab-owned stud farms. Eighteenth-century Georgian houses. The Boyne Valley. Ruins of Cistercian monasteries. The Donkey Sanctuary. And several thousand ordinary families living in the towns and villages, in crumbling cottages and brash new bungalows, along those silent roads. The Midlands. Sometimes called the back of beyond.

But someone had thoughtfully added a stabilizing alloy to the material, to keep it from blowing up inconveniently. The Irish media called it a godsend.

In a bizarre coincidence, Father McGurk's sister Agnes suffered a fatal heart attack in her car, forty miles away, right around the time of the accident. The police found a container of highly enriched uranium in the boot, and in her purse several primitive diagrams, based on 1950s technology, showing how to build a hydrogen bomb.

About a month later, Sean Harrison died of radiation sickness. At first, officials thought the cause might have been some contaminated metal he had imported from Russia, for use in soft-drink cans. But this report caused a seismic tremor in the stock market. Shares of Harrison companies, already volatile, dropped sharply, setting off a wave of panic selling on three continents. The police hastily announced that there was no truth at all to the irresponsible rumors about contaminated metal. They were following other, more plausible, leads. So far, though, they haven't come up with anything.

Ludo? Ludo. His helicopter never landed at Kyteler Manor that day. I like to think he looked down at the moment I crashed his silver car, then seized the controls and flew the chopper like a maniac straight under the bridge. When he understood all of what happened, he did what he had to do: drove on. Spirit of the Event.

Come to think of it, before I lost consciousness, I did hear a roar. Deafening. With music.

In any case, he had his beautiful red Giulietta ti waiting for him in London. It's a closed car; it would do him for the winter.

One last thing. I've recently heard some news of Princess Victoria Anne. That insane plan of hers—to do New York, London, and Washington in one go—is still on. I'll resist saying very Mutch so. She has decided to eliminate middle men altogether, take a more hands-on approach from here on. There are reliable people working directly with her, notably a fabulously wealthy widow who has excellent contacts in the third world. Vicky was traveling as Zan Playfair when they met. In adjacent seats, while flying first class.